MURDER
OF
CROWS

N GRAY

By N Gray

Scout Thorne
The Secret Tomb
Murder of Crows

Blaire Thorne
Ulysses Exposed
Voodoo Priest
Butterflies and Hurricanes
Salvation
Underworld Legacy

Shifter Days, Vampire Nights, & Demons in Between
Twisted
Lady Hawk and Her Mountain Man
Hidden Shifter
Wolf
Wolf Retreat
Night Hunter
The Fixer
Kai
Lee
Flynn
Jude

www.ngraybooks.com

Vinci Books

vinci-books.com

Published by Vinci Books Ltd in 2025

1

A CIP catalogue record for this book is available from the British Library.
Paperback ISBN: 9781036702168

The EU GPSR authorised representative is Logos Europe, 9 rue Nicolas Poussion, 17000 La Rochelle, France
contact@logoseurope.eu

Chapter One

"What do you mean Antarctica?" I said, not understanding how River arrived there or who had left him there. He had disappeared while we were in the Underworld. Him being in Antarctica made little sense.

"The same reason, Scout," Dad said with a hint of sarcasm. "The person responsible for wanting me dead wanted River out of the way."

"But why?"

"Because together, he and I are stronger."

I pursed my lips. Someone wanted my father dead, and it wasn't just the assistant. Someone had hired the assistant to do his dirty work for him. I shook my head in shame. I'd been so focused on River and his disappearance that I didn't ask Victor if he ever found out who had started it all.

"Do you know who tried to destroy you?"

Mom stood closer, folding her arms across her chest. She stopped near my left-hand side and slightly in front of me in a protective stance. I didn't think she wanted me to leave with Victor again, and suspected every time he visited a trigger reaction occurred and she became a fussy-mother-hen over me. I didn't blame her, each time he took me away from her, it was for long periods of time.

"I thought you said you shared your power with River and now with me. Do we take power away from you, or does it just double?" I needed to understand what Vic meant and the only way was to ask like a five-year-old.

Victor rounded his shoulders, and his eyes flitted from Ralph to Mom, and then to me. He exhaled a breath, and I suspected he'd filled that sigh with annoyance.

"I've never shared this with anyone," he said gravely, staring down at me with intense eyes. "And if either of you," he pointed at Mom and Ralph, "say a word to anyone, I will destroy you."

"Stop threatening my family," I said, grabbing his index finger and lowering his hand. "Nobody will say anything. Now tell us." I was about to roll my eyes when Dad's features turned sinisterly and then returned to his devilish human demeanor.

"Whomever I share my power with doubles my power, and when we use it together, it's that much more powerful. My brothers and sisters hate that I can do this because none of them can."

"You mean they can't share their powers with anyone?" I asked, intrigued.

"No," Vic said, his shoulders dropping slightly. "And because of this, I always have a target on my back."

"Would your family hurt you?" Mom asked.

"Definitely. Seth tried to kill me when I was an infant. Our sister almost drowned me. But the point is, it could be either of them or something else entirely who used the Mask of Immortality against me. And now they have River..." he fell silent for a moment. His metallic armor twinkled as the shadows from the branches and leaves moved across his chest like ghostly fingers trying to touch him.

The waterfall in the distance slapped harder against the water's surface, pulling my attention away from Victor. I leaned on my left leg and peered around Father's broad shoulders and black wings and flinched.

A mermaid sat beneath the spray of the waterfall and washed his body. He had long, knotted hair and large, dark eyes. When he glanced up, he smiled; his enormous mouth had sharp teeth, and he blew a kiss before diving into the water.

"Scout?" Victor said, pulling me back into the present.

"Yeah?" I glanced up and smiled.

Victor glanced over his shoulder. "What are you looking at?"

"Just the mermaid who was there." I pointed at the spot where he was.

"Don't antagonize the water creatures, they don't play fair." He warned. "Anyway, you need to go to Antarctica—"

"No," Mom said, with anger in her voice. "I forbid it."

"Mom," I said, crossing the distance between us and wrapping my arms around her shoulders. "I'll be fine. You know I'll be fine, and you know I must do this."

"Why can't you go?" she asked Victor, ignoring me, but she still put her arms around me and squeezed me tightly against her body.

"You know I don't do well with humans or other supernaturals."

Mom snorted. "Yeah, true, especially with your temper tantrums."

I glanced up to see Dad's features morph into his more evil look, and then he calmed down.

"See, you can't even handle me teasing you."

"Exactly, Blaire, I have demons who do the dirty work for me."

"Does that include your own daughter—"

"Mom!"

She patted my shoulder. "It's okay, honey. The adults are having a conversation."

I pushed away from her and stood beside Dad.

"You know she wants to find River, so I'm giving her the opportunity. If I send my demons to find him, they always cause chaos. The last thing we need is another war between us or worse, they kill River. This way, if Scout goes by herself, she'll do so quietly."

"I'll be okay, Mom, I promise." I smiled, but she wasn't looking at me. She was glaring daggers at Dad.

"I hate this, Scout. You aren't ready to do all this by yourself."

"I know you want to keep me safe, but you know I can handle anything that comes my way."

She glanced at me, cocking her head to the side, and raised an eyebrow.

"If you aren't back by the end of the week, we'll join you and phone me every single day, or I'm flying out there to bring you home."

"Fine," I said. But what I didn't say was I'd do anything not to have her in my face while trying to do something on my own. My mom meant well, but sometimes her love smothered me.

She gave me a long hug and kissed my cheek. Ralph hugged me too and patted the top of my head; I swiped his hand away before he could do that a second time.

"Ready?" Dad asked, holding out his elbow for me to take.

"Sure," I took his arm, and we walked together toward the lagoon. We approached the lapping crystal-blue water when three heads popped up, each mermaid smiling. But instead of entering the water, we stepped out onto the freezing snow.

Chapter Two

"Dad, you forgot to stop for winter clothing for me," I said. My teeth chattering as I hugged myself. A snowflake floated in front of my face and settled on my hand. The pretty patterns were crystal clear with the sun behind me.

"Here," he said, snapping his fingers and handing me a large thick coat, warm pants, fluffy socks, and boots equipped for slippery snow. "Over there is the town," he pointed in the distance. I squinted, but all I saw was white. "But be careful. They don't take kindly to supernaturals. And..." He left his word hanging.

"What?" I asked nervously. "And what?" I pulled on the jacket, and I sighed as it warmed me instantly.

"There's a reason we don't come here," he started. "The residents don't want supernaturals in their space, so hide your talents."

"What do you mean?" I asked, the lines between my brows deepening.

"They've lived here for a while and that's just the kind of tribe they are. Call your crows to guide and protect you."

"What?" I said, feeling even more confused than I did a few moments ago. "Why must I call my crows?" I asked and, in my head, called out to Jake, the leader of my crows and my spirit animals. He'd be here as soon as he could.

"You'll see," he said with a smile, "but they're harmless unless they feel threatened. So don't threaten them. Just go in there, look for River and get out again. It should be that easy."

"Well, that sounds easy enough," I said sarcastically and glanced in the general direction of the town, but only saw snow. "Are you going to wait for me?"

"No, I'm still investigating who started this mess, and I have demons to torture," he said sinisterly. His smile widening that much more, frightening me. I did not want to be on the receiving end of his harsh treatment.

I opened my mouth to ask another question when the air popped in my face, and he disappeared. "Blasted," I mumbled to myself and started dressing, placing my other clothing in the bag that Dad had left. "Damn, it's cold."

I trudged through the thick snow, each step I took, my legs sunk deeper into the soft white ice. My lungs burned with each breath I took and although the clothing Victor had given me could be worn in freezing conditions, I was cold and wet. Luckily, my feet remained warm and dry in the fluffy socks and boots.

The hike up the hill felt like it took me forever. The sun stayed bright and would continue shining for another month when the sun sets completely for six months.

I rounded an ice boulder when the tips of buildings came into view, along with smoke coming out of chimneys.

Exhausted from the hike, I choked up with happiness. I was one step closer to finding River and then we could get out of here.

'Why couldn't Victor just leave me here instead of dropping me all the way over there?' I thought to myself as I passed the town sign that read

White Devil Hills, Antarctica, EST 1779, POP 999.

The name was fitting for the snowy conditions; it was an utter pain in the bum to get here though. It was the population numbers that left an unpleasant taste in my mouth and hoped it was now 1001 now that River and I were here.

Once I passed the sign and my boots struck a hard, flat road, I continued the path toward the town that sat between two majestic mountains. Not wanting to miss anything, I stopped to admire the scenery, taking a snapshot with my cell phone.

I stared at the rocky mountains on either side of the town that seemed to arch inward slightly, as if it cupped the town. It reminded me of hands protecting something special. I cupped my hands in front of my mouth to warm my fingers and blew into them; my breath was a cloud in front of me then disappearing just as quickly.

The town itself looked large enough for at least two-thousand people, even though it was only half of that. There was one enormous building in the middle of it I assumed was a hotel, which was strange for a small town here where there were little tourists. Then, surrounding the hotel were double- and single-story homes with smaller containers between them. There was a main road going straight through and out the other side. I couldn't see whether the road ended or if it carried on beyond the ice wall.

One thing I noticed the town did not have was a church or a chapel. There was nothing that screamed religion was being taught here like one would usually see in a town. And on the right-hand side of the town stood a frozen pond with trees circling half of it on the far right-hand side. I found it strange that trees grew here considering it snowed all year round.

"Can I help you, miss?"

I flinched and spun around, coming face-to-chest with a large man. He wore a tweed jacket with a waistcoat and black pants tucked into snow boots. I glanced up to see his face, but his hoody bathed him in darkness.

"Um, hi, I'm looking for someone." I wrinkled my nose and stepped away from the man to put some distance between us. The stench of his smoke-filled clothing stole my breath, and I sucked in fresh air.

"Well, miss, you're very far from home." He removed his hoody, revealing his youthful face. He glanced over his shoulder, then back at me. "How did you get here? Never mind," he said with knitted brows, and not waiting for me to answer. "I don't think anyone in town is waiting for a visitor," he said and smiled, revealing sharp, rotten teeth.

I took another small step backward and to the side so that it looked like I was just standing at an angle instead of trying to get out of his rancid breath.

"I've been told my friend is here and I would like to find him. Perhaps you've heard of a man named River—"

"No," he said, shaking his head. "There's no man named River, but...," he said, pinching his sharp chin with his index finger and thumb. His eyes rolled to the left, then the right, before focusing on me once more. It was unnerving to witness, like his eyes were loose inside his head or didn't quite fit him.

I took the time to look at this strange man. His hair was short and disheveled, three-day stubble on his jaw, and strange colored eyes; they weren't blue or green but dark in-between. He was an entire head and shoulders taller than me, with powerful hands. If I had to take a guess, I'd say his large hands could snap a bone in two with little force.

"A lost man arrived a few weeks ago not knowing his name," he continued. "It's been so long it feels as though he's already one of us."

"Oh," I said, sounding sadder than I wanted to. Something else must've happened to River if he didn't know his name, and hoped he would trust me enough to bring him back home for medical attention. I glanced at the town and then at the man, stepping slightly to the side and a little away from him. "Do you know where he is?"

"Ol Henry took him under his wing and gave him a job at the hotel bar," he said, pointing at the largest building I'd correctly guessed was a hotel. "Would you like me to accompany you there?" His eyes rolled to the left, then right, before settling on me again.

"Uh, sure," I said with a smile. "I'd love that. Then you can tell me all about the town and how long you've lived there." I started walking toward the town.

"Do you really want to know about my town?" he asked earnestly.

"Yes, of course," I said, still smiling at him. The more I understood about this town, the better it was for River and me.

"I haven't shared that with anybody in so long," he said, catching up to me. He swung a fishing rod and rope I hadn't noticed before over his shoulder and walked beside me.

I glanced at the man's back and noticed someone had roughly sewed the hoody to the tweed jacket. It was primitive yet neat. He reminded me of an explorer-librarian.

"My name is Scout," I offered.

"Neville," he said. His smile reached his eyes as he faced forward and walked at a brisk pace. "I can't remember the exact date I arrived or where I'd been, only that this place had always meant to be my home. And come to think of it, I don't remember having parents either. I only remember my days from that first day when I walked this path, much like we're doing now."

I glanced behind me at the path, which disappeared around a bend. "Where did you come from now?" I asked. "Were you fishing?" I jerked my chin at the rod over his shoulder.

"What, this?" He held up a piece of the rope and tapped the fishing rod. "Nah, no fishing here. What is fishing?" He furrowed his brows.

"We use a fishing rod, like the one you're holding now, to catch fish that swim in water. And then we cook and eat the fish."

"Oh, that, well no, I don't use this for fish, nor do I think we have fish in the pond."

When he didn't elaborate, I continued, "What did you use the rod for?"

"Back there is... uh... to feed the well." He moved the fishing rod to his other side so that I couldn't see it properly.

"What do you feed in the well?"

"The folks here are very nice. We're quiet, down to earth, and hard workers," he said, ignoring my question. He remained quiet as the wind kicked up a notch, blowing through my short hair and making me shiver. "But we don't hurt anyone." He blurted.

I didn't know how to respond, so thought it best to keep quiet.

"It's very peaceful here. You'll enjoy it."

"Do you work?"

"No, I only feed the well."

I tried glancing at the hand that was far away from me, but Neville kept it hidden. Something caught my eye and when I glanced over my shoulder, it was a red dot mixing with the snow.

"Nobody is lonely here," he said, pulling my attention to him.

"What do you do for fun?" I asked, changing the subject.

"We play games," he said, glancing over his shoulder. He quickened his steps, and I jogged to keep up. "Come, the snow is getting closer."

I shivered and huddled into my jacket. A breeze scratched my face, and I turned around; in the distance, large gray clouds formed and grew, and they were heading our way. The ominous clouds seemed to grow angrier with sparks of lightning brightening the darkening sky.

"Hurry," he said, breaking out into a sprint. He gripped the fishing rod and rope tighter against his body and ran.

I chased after Neville, but he was too quick, leaving me behind. The clouds behind me grew larger and blacker and approached with such speed I almost stopped to watch the spectacle. But something told me not to stop, to keep running for shelter.

I chased after Neville, but the wind slapped hard against my exposed skin, leaving it cold and raw. The snow and wind whipped around me, blocking my view of Neville and the town. I stopped running and walked, bracing myself against the harsh elements of the weather. I felt myself leaning forward, clasping my jacket, and pushed forward.

"Neville?" I yelled as I covered my face with one hand. "Neville?" I called again, but all I heard was the howling wind. The last thing I needed was to be buried in a blizzard. "Neville?" I cried out one last time as hope disappeared in a puddle at my cold feet.

I flinched when an arm grabbed mine and yanked me to the left. The door slammed shut in my face. The wind outside scratched against the container door and howled menacingly as it passed. I shuddered at the thought of being caught in the snowstorm and relieved I'd met Neville even though he was strange.

"Scout?" Neville said. "Are you okay? That was a close one. We never go outside when the White Devil is out there."

I slowly turned to face Neville, but I didn't notice him; my eyes bounced around the room as I took it all in. The masks. Heads. Hairy bodies. There were four heads mounted on plaques for all to see. All the animals he'd stuffed. So many defenseless animals.

"This is my home," he said proudly.

"I thought we were going to the hotel?" I stepped closer to the door and reached for the handle.

"No!" he yelled, making me jump. "We can't go outside now," he said. His tone was gentler, but he still frightened me. "It was a good thing my place is the first house as you enter town." Neville smiled, but there was something in his eyes I couldn't make out. "When the White Devil is gone, I'll take you there. It's a short distance up the road, but not now. No," he shook his head, "not now. I can't take you now. Nobody is ever out now."

"How long is the White Devil usually out?"

"About an hour."

If Neville wanted to keep me company in his house for an hour, I could do that. It was a small room, but perfect for one person. And even though Neville was weird with a strange eye twitch and animal heads on his walls, I had Father's power. I would use it against him, even though Victor had warned me not to use it here.

Neville disappeared behind a small curtain and returned, wearing a cardigan with an empty pipe in his mouth. He packed wood in the fireplace and lit it; heat engulfed the small room immediately and my body stung from the sudden change in temperature.

"Come sit," he said, patting the only available space beside him. "It's warm here."

I patted my knife in its sheath and approached the two-seater couch.

Chapter Three

"We all have something to do in town," Neville said, now standing near his fireplace. "I feed the well once a week, Mikey chops trees for wood," he pointed to the side, and I assumed it was his neighbor who was Mikey, "and Miss Harriet bakes bread." He scrunched his face as if to say her baking wasn't as great as it sounded.

"Are those your jobs?"

His response was a confused expression. I needed to ask better questions so that he could understand me. "When you say you all have something to do, are you paid to do that, or is that just what you do to keep busy?"

"It's what we do to keep busy. We all help around the town, and some even have rooms with windows on the main road, making it easier for us to get things for headaches or something nice for our home."

I assumed the reference to rooms with windows were shops.

"So there's no exchange of money to pay for food,

water, or electricity?" I asked, looking at the light switch that was made to look like fire.

He furrowed his brows, and I took that as a no.

I stood and walked to the other side of the room, brushing my fingers along the curtain that separated the large room from his tiny bedroom. In the far corner was a counter with a bread knife and chopping board, and in the other corner was another curtain for his shower and toilet.

"What's money?" Neville finally asked, still looking confused.

"It's what we use to pay for the goods or services we need. But from what you've said, everyone shares what they created or got from nature."

Neville nodded, but the confusion in his eyes told me he didn't fully understand the concept. Then he pointed at the beak of a bird. "We only have crows here and this little guy kept stealing my bread," he said, changing the subject.

Shocked, I stared at the poor winged creature stuck on Neville's wall. I silently called out to Jake once more and said that they should be careful when approaching the town; someone could hunt them.

"What else do you do around here?" I asked. "What I mean is, what's the purpose of your town?"

Neville was quiet for a while and coughed a few times. "The elders have been here much longer than anyone else and they protect the sacred land. While the rest of us ensure the people of our town get what they need to survive," he said matter-of-factly and sat in his chair near the fire again.

When the room filled with silence, I hurried to the door and opened it.

"What's wrong?" He yelled, jumping up from his chair and dashing to me, pushing the door shut before I could see outside. "Not yet," he shook his head, "wait."

"Why?" I said, trying to push his thick arm away from the door so I could open it again. "The storm is over."

"Wait," he said with pleading eyes.

I hesitantly lowered my arms. "Why, Neville?" I said softer, gentler, so he could hear my desperation. "I need to go to the hotel and find River."

"You need to wait." He raised his hand to shush me, pressing his ear against the door, and spoke, yet no sound came out of his mouth.

I flinched when a sinister howl blew past the house, making all the hairs on my arms stand up. Neville pinched his eyes closed and continued mumbling silently. I wanted to ask if he was praying, but something told me to wait; the concentration on his face was alarming.

Another sinister howl sounded, but closer to the door this time. I shivered and the hairs on the back of my neck stood on end, making me hug myself. I didn't know what that sound was, or which creature made it, only that I didn't want to get too close to it.

Neville closed his eyes, his hand squeezing the door handle. The wind whistled past and then... silence as the lights flickered off and back on. Neville removed his hand and stood tall, exhaling a deep breath. His pupils had dilated, and his face had paled. His eyes flitted to me as if seeing me for the first time and smiled, but it didn't reach his eyes.

"Okay," he said, nodding. "We can go." He grabbed his coat, opened the door, and a gust of wind smacked me in the face.

I huddled into myself again and followed him outside. The moment we stepped outside, everyone exited their homes, waving happily at each other as if for the first time, and headed for the hotel.

Neville waved at a man with bright red hair and beard. He wore a thick red and black flannel shirt and black pants. All he needed now was an axe to complete the lumberjack look.

"That's Mikey," Neville said without looking my way. "And that's Miss Harriet." She must've heard him and glanced our way, her eyes flitting between Neville and me, and her smile brightened. Her white hair was up in a bun, and she pushed her golden rimmed glasses up her nose. Her light pink top had a picture of a cat across her chest and stomach.

"Hello Neville, who is your friend?" Miss Harriet asked when she neared. She continued staring at me as we headed for the hotel.

"This is…" Neville glanced my way nervously, as if he'd already forgotten my name.

I thought I'd help him out and proffered my hand. "Hi, I'm Scout," I said. When she ignored my hand, I placed my hand back inside the pocket where it was warmer, and I pretended not to be embarrassed.

"What are you doing here?" she asked, the lines between her eyes deepening. Now that she was so close, I noticed there was no glass in her frames.

"She's looking for…" Neville glanced my way again.

"River," I said to him, then glanced at Miss Harriet. "I'm looking for River. Neville tells me he's working at the hotel."

"Ah yes," she said, thinking. "I remember the newcomer. He got here a couple of weeks ago, not knowing where the hell he was. Yes, yes," she mumbled, deep in thought, "he's a very nice guy. Where do you know him from?"

"Back home," I said, not really in the mood to go

through my life story with strangers, and not knowing what would happen if they knew more about our lives.

"And where is home?" she asked.

I cringed internally, unsure of what to say. Even though I didn't know them, I doubted they knew where I even came from. "Sterling Meadow. Have you heard of it?"

"Nope," she said, glancing at Neville. "I don't think either of us has."

"Nope," Neville confirmed, shaking his head. "Here we are." He pointed at something.

I turned to see what he was referring to and stopped; the hotel seemed larger than it did a moment ago. I craned my head up and counted at least fifty stories. When I first approached the town, the hotel didn't look like it was more than ten stories high, yet now it seemed to go on into the clouds that had gathered.

"What are you waiting for?" Neville asked impatiently. He and Miss Harriet waited for me on the corner of the black wrap-around porch.

I ignored him as my eyes bounced across the various dark windows on the floors until I found the name; *Tainted Souls Hotel*. My breath caught in my throat as the cold enveloped me and goosebumps popped along my arms. The dark wall seemed to cry tears of fear as the lines moved up and down. The gargoyles on each corner of each floor screamed in silent agony as their eyes followed my every move. And the energy vibrating off the walls bounced back and into me like static electricity. They had charged this building with an evil current.

I'd been to the Underworld, and I'd seen various levels within my father's realm—even an ocean—and I'd seen demons, but this place was something else. It was... stained... tarnished... infected... contaminated... I couldn't quite place what kind of evil lived here, only that it made me worry. My father was Lord of the Underworld, yet he didn't want to enter this town. Unless there were restrictions someone had placed on him from going anywhere near this place—which I doubted. I understood he had to find the person responsible for everything that had gone wrong, but he'd teleported us so far out of town he had to have another reason. And like always, there were things he conveniently left out.

"Scout?" Miss Harriet said, now close to me, and squeezed my arm. "Are you all right, dear?" she asked sincerely. I hadn't noticed her walk back to me and blinked at her. "You've gone whiter than you were before."

I swallowed the lump in my throat and, as much as I didn't want to enter the hotel, I had to. I had to find River and then get the hell out of this place.

"I'm fine." I managed to say and swallowed again. "Lead the way."

The other residents flocked toward the hotel, with us trailing in last. It amazed me everyone could fit but when we entered; we were the only ones in the lobby.

"Where did everyone go?" I asked, glancing around. To the left of the lobby stood a set of closed, blue doors with a plaque above reading *Nightmare Hall*. To the right was another set of open red doors and on the plaque above read *Toxic Bar - Choose Your Poison*. I didn't want to enter either room.

"He should be here," Neville said, heading toward the bar.

"Crap," I mumbled to myself, but followed.

Someone stepped out from behind a half-closed door near reception with hard lines on his face. The man reminded me of a seasoned biker who smashed everything in his way with his forehead and, for some reason, he thought I was the cockroach he wanted to squash as he scowled at me. He folded his arms across his large chest, revealing the tattoos on the lower parts of his forearms; on his right arm it read; "MAKE" and on the left, "ME". Not wanting to aggravate the man or his arms, I ran after Neville and Miss Harriet, happy to be in their company.

I jogged inside the bar behind Neville and Miss Harriet and almost smacked into the back of them. "Sorry," I whispered, correcting my footing. I smiled sweetly when Miss Harriet glanced over her shoulder at me, but it was the furniture inside the bar that caught my attention. They had made the tables and chairs out of bones that were dyed various colors of deep red to deep purple. The cushions on the chairs were leather, and from the way the material stretched, I guessed they were human skin instead of animal hide.

I swallowed, as the knot in my stomach threatened to explode out of my mouth when the smell of a wet animal with a hint of ale wafted in the air. I surveyed the area and wished my entrance didn't make a noise. Everyone sitting at the tables near the entrance stared at me like I was dinner. Quickly, I squeezed myself between Neville and Miss Harriet, slipping my arms through theirs, and we approached the bar like one body.

The bartender turned around to ask us what we wanted to drink, and River stared at me, dumbstruck. He cocked his head to the side, then straight again while cleaning the glass in his hand. "What can I get you?" he asked, still staring at me.

"River?" I unhooked my arms and stepped out in front of the other two, pushing chairs aside, and leaning my elbows on the leather counter, cringing while doing so. "Do you remember me?" I asked, silently hoping when he saw me it would jog his memory.

River stared at me, through me, unseeing. He blinked and shook his head. "Uh, no, who are you?" He arched an eyebrow.

Although I knew River had no memory it still hurt hearing his words; that a man I had dated for a long time saying he didn't know me cut more than I'd wanted.

"It's me, Scout." I reached for his hand, but he pulled away. I knew he wasn't rejecting me, he was uncertain about me, therefore I tried not to take his actions personally. "You worked for my father... and we were close. Do you remember anything?"

River coughed into his hand and wiped the phlegm on his pants; although his pants were black, I caught hints of red.

"What did they do to you?" I whispered, standing back, happy to no longer be touching the sticky leather counter.

"I don't know what you're talking about. I came here," River said, raising his hands gesturing at the bar, "to work."

"No, you didn't. Someone put you here on purpose, and I need to find out why." I leaned forward again and whispered, "And you're ill."

River glanced around nervously, ensuring the two people behind me stayed there, and leaned forward. "How do you know?"

"I was there when it happened."

Chapter Four

We sat in a corner at the back of the bar, each having our backs to a wall and our line of sight on both exits; it's one of those defense mechanisms we had learned while fighting monsters. I played with the red paper serviette in my hands while River sipped on his ale, an ale I did not want to taste. It smelled like sulphur.

Neville and Miss Harriet left me to join their friends at a different table, allowing River and me some privacy. Occasionally, Neville looked at us and smiled when I noticed his stares.

River combed his fingers through his hair and stretched his back before sitting upright, leaving his drink to give me his attention. "Would you like to start from the beginning?"

The tone of his voice was gentle, reminding me of the time we spent together. We were so busy with my father's work that some days we barely had time for ourselves. But when it was just us, River showered me with kisses, hugs, naughty things, and late-night whispers that revealed his true heart. For a fire-breathing-skeleton, he was more human than most. I missed those times, and I missed him. He had a tender way about him that only I saw, and I saw it again with him now.

"What do you remember?" I asked.

"I remember walking in snow and following the path to this place. Everything else is just... darkness."

I nodded my understanding. "Okay, I'll be as concise as possible, and if you want more detail, I'll give it to you." I glanced around, ensuring nobody heard us. "Now don't let this scare you... my father is Lord of the Underworld, and you work for him. You turn into a ball of angry flames and help him collect contracts for their souls." I waited for his response, but he just stared at me. I took that as a sign to carry on. "Someone tried to kill him, and he asked for our help. We saved him, but they hurt you in the process and you disappeared for three weeks. Today my father fetched me and said I could find you here. So, I'm here to bring you home."

River stared at me like I'd grown horns, but I knew he was busy processing the information.

"What about my life before working for your dad?"

"You had a normal human life and then you signed a contract with my dad to save your mother's life."

River blinked at me and sat back, staring at the others who were laughing, eating, drinking, and enjoying their conversations. The bar area had filled up substantially in the last five minutes, and it didn't look like anyone was leaving. It amazed me there was enough space.

"Is it always this busy?" I asked, feeling slightly claustrophobic.

"It's dinnertime," he said absentmindedly, then turned to look at me. He sniffed and quickly held his head back while pinching his nose. "My nose keeps bleeding." He quickly wiped his nose with the red serviette I handed him and glanced around nervously.

"Do you feel drained or ill?"

"Honestly, I don't feel great, and losing blood every day all day is catching up with me." He wiped the last bit of blood and pocketed the serviette. "It's not safe for me here when it happens."

I glanced around but nobody paid us any attention. "Are there any doctors here who can help?"

"When I first arrived, Henry suggested I see someone, but I never had the time. And if what you said is correct, I don't think a doctor can help here. I'll need something a little more magical." He smiled, but it didn't reach his tired eyes. In the time I'd known River, he never had dark rings under his eyes, or looked as sickly as he did now.

I smiled sadly, agreeing with him. "That may be a bit difficult. I hear they don't like supernaturals?"

"No," he said wearily. "They don't."

"Are you able to sleep?"

"No, little to none."

"Do you just work here, or do you work somewhere else, too?"

"I work in the bar daily, and I help Henry when he needs someone to work at reception."

"Is Henry the guy with the tattoos on his lower arms?"

"He's actually a nice guy."

"He seems pretty scary to me." As much as I didn't want to admit it but Henry scared me, and few monsters or humans did; which said a lot about Henry.

"If you're as tough as I think you are, then you should consider him a puppy."

I harrumphed. "If you say so." I almost rolled my eyes.

"So, what are we going to do, or should we leave and find someone who can help me in the Underworld?"

I hadn't thought about that. Father had said I should find River and get out, but I couldn't help but think there was another reason they had sent River here in the first place. And with Father searching for those responsible for this mess, I doubted he could help River with whatever was wrong with him. We needed to find an alternative.

I glanced at River and watched him watch everyone. He even combed his hair in a different direction than he used to, and it was then I noticed a clump of hair on the side closest to me was missing. He kept touching his nose in case it was bleeding again, but it wasn't now. Things weren't going great for him; his hair was falling out, wasn't sleeping much, and he had no memory. He needed someone more powerful than a doctor and a witch to help him.

My father needed his flaming skeleton back so the two of them could continue collecting souls as payment or, as my father would say, his world would end. He could be overly dramatic sometimes and this was when I'd roll my eyes, but never where he could see it.

No, I selfishly needed River; the man I fell in love with back and in one piece. And although he and I were no longer a couple, we were friends, and I would do everything in my power to help him.

Glass smashed, tearing my attention away from River and toward the bar area. Someone had dropped a glass somewhere and nobody moved out of the way or attempted to clean it up. Everyone continued talking and drinking the ale like nothing had happened.

When my eyes fell upon the man with the tattoos, my back stiffened. He stood behind the bar, but instead of serving customers, he stared at me. Nervously, I grabbed River's hand.

"Ow," he said, yanking his hand back.

"Why is Henry staring at me like that?" I asked, desperately not wanting to take my eyes off him but also afraid that I now had his full attention.

"Huh? Oh, that's just what he does. I was their first newcomer in years and I'm assuming it's a bit of a shock for them to have two newcomers so soon after one another."

"What should I do? Break eye contact or go over and buy him a drink?"

"Definitely introduce yourself." River pushed his chair back and grabbed my hand. "Come on, he really is harmless."

"He doesn't look it."

"I think he was a biker in his previous life."

'Ha! Which life?' I thought.

We approached Henry casually, but deep inside, I was dying. I was in a strange town where the residents had weird moving eyes. I didn't know anyone, and River probably couldn't channel his dangerous fire if I were in trouble. If anything happened, I would have to use my powers, and I didn't think it would go down well here.

"Henry, this is my friend, Scout," River said, introducing us. "She says my name is River."

The hard lines on Henry's face softened a smidge and one side of his mouth curled upward in a half-smile. "River, you say. It suits you better than Boy," Henry said, biting off the end of a cigar and smoking it, but without lighting it. "I'm Henry, owner of this wonderful hotel in this Hell Hole." He proffered a hand.

"Nice to meet you," I said, shaking his warm hand, and

pleasantly surprised he didn't squeeze hard. "Does the whole town fit inside the bar?"

Henry smiled, and it reached his hungry eyes. "Yes, a town that eats together lives longer."

I wasn't sure that was the saying, but I wasn't about to tell him otherwise. "What does the town eat?" I asked, hoping what was on the menu was something I could chew on.

"Liquid diet, I'm afraid," Henry said, excusing himself to help someone on the other side of the bar.

"What does that mean?" I asked River.

"You'll see," he said and went behind the bar.

"Should I be afraid?"

"No, it's nothing to worry about. It's not like they're cannibals."

I stared wide eyed at him, swallowed hard, and moved closer to the wall and bar area in case I needed a quick escape out the back entrance. I glanced at the door behind the bar and hoped it was an exit.

I faced the growing crowd of townsfolk and hoped whatever was about to happen didn't involve munching on me. When a bell tolled, ice filled my veins, and I hugged myself.

"Don't look so worried," River said, patting my shoulder, "I'll be right back."

I opened my mouth to ask him where he was going, but he had already disappeared, the door behind the bar area swinging closed.

I flinched when a man with a hawk nose knocked on the bar counter, staring at me, but spoke to Henry and ordered an ale. He smiled, revealing missing teeth. When he blinked, his eyes also seemed lost in their sockets as they rolled slightly to the left and then to the right before correcting themselves to stare at me once more.

A nervousness flooded my system, and I called out to Jake, the leader of my crows. There was still silence on his end, and I hoped they were on their way and staying out of the townsfolk's view. I'd hate to have any of my crows mounted on a wall here for eternity.

I was about to follow River when the door opened, and he carried a tray with glasses filled with a thick red liquid. River placed the tray on the bar counter, unloaded the glasses, and exited again. He did this a few times until it filled the bar counter, with Henry placing the filled glasses in neat rows.

Then, as if by magic, the townsfolk moved as one. They formed a long, winding row that snaked throughout the bar area. Then, one by one, they each took a glass and moved out of the way for the next person to take a glass. I watched quietly as they did their little dance of fetch and get out of the way.

River and Henry watched as well; Henry smoked his unlit cigar with his large arms folded, revealing his tattoos, and River leaned against the counter that held the various bottles of ale.

When the last person picked up their glass, again as one, they raised the hand holding the red liquid. They spoke without making a sound, reminding me of Neville while we had waited for the White Devil wind to end.

I recoiled when they chanted loudly, "Praise the White Devil for protecting us and shielding us from the outside world. With this hand, we raise your praises. Our cups will never empty, for you always provide. And with our lips, we'll drink from your vein. Our souls forever yours." And then they downed the proverbial cool-aid.

What happened next felt dreamlike, surreal, and definitely not human. For a town who prided themselves for not liking supernaturals, it surprised me to witness them shedding their human skins. At the drop of a hat, their skins, wigs, and clothing fell from their actual bodies and beneath that were the monsters I read about. Monsters no human could ever conjure up. The monsters from our nightmares, and the monsters from the Underworld.

Chapter Five

"What the—" I started when River slapped his hand over my mouth.

I wanted to protest, but River grunted next to my ear, "If you want to live, don't say another word." I nodded and blinked. River slowly released his tight hold on me.

"What the hell is going on?" I whispered. "Is this a cult, a monster rally, or something sinister?" I doubted anything could be more sinister than a monster rally, but then again, I knew nothing about monster rallies.

"Definitely something else," River said softly. "I may not remember who I am or what happened to me before I arrived here, but I seem to understand monsters, and they are no different." He jerked his chin in their direction, "Remember, if you leave them alone, they'll pretty much go on about their day and leave you alone."

"Why didn't you warn me?"

"It's hard to describe," he said, glancing from me to the monsters while they drank their non-vegan-gummy-juice.

"Are they skinless vampires or..." I couldn't finish my

sentence as I stared at the town's-monsters. With their human skins around their ankles, they revealed their smooth, scaly-looking skins; they were pale with bloody blotches and dark veins running just beneath the surface reminding me of maps. Their heads were smooth, and their eyes were dark orbs, which explained why their other "human" eyes seemed to roll inside their heads. I wondered how they saw through the fake ones.

I couldn't help staring and was grateful nobody paid any attention to me. Their real eyes reminded me of fisheyes, but instead of it being on the sides of their heads, it was in front; where normal eyes were meant to be. Their noses reminded me of a bat's; two large, lance-shaped noses, and their mouths were big and sharp and toothy, while their fingers were long, sharp talons.

And since I didn't fully understand what kind of creature they were, I had no way of telling if they were male or female. They were just monsters with no sex organs to tell them apart. If there was a gun to my head and I had to guess what these creatures were, they were a mix between the Underworld demons and vampires.

The Underworld demons were usually lava filled, dark —sometimes smooth-skinned—creatures with an insatiable hunger to eat humans. If hurt, they sometimes bled lava, or their pores smoked, or exhibited some other trick. Each demon had something different about them, with a different way to destroy them. What these creatures had in common with demons was they had no hair and they had black, beady eyes. And wafting in the surrounding air was sulphur; that typically filled the corridors of the Underworld. But where demons could physically change into a human, these monsters slipped on human-like skin.

I assumed from the aroma assaulting my nostrils the

cool-aid they drank was blood, and vampires loved blood. Where vampires drank blood from willing humans or from their dying victims. These creatures sipped from their glasses like it was Holy Communion. I didn't know what their chanting meant before they downed their drink, but it left me on edge.

Once the noise settled down, the townsfolk pulled up their skin and clothing, fixed their eyes and wigs, and continued like nothing had happened. For most of them, they needed to adjust their skin so that it stuck to their demon flesh beneath, or it would just hang or fold in places; especially around the jawline and hands.

Then, one by one, they left, and the crowd lessened. When it was only a handful left and us, Henry disappeared to tend to a bell tolling in the foyer and River served ale to a customer.

I stood squashed in the corner near the bar and slowly unlatched my fingers from the grooves in the walls and the tension between my shoulders seeped away. My back and neck muscles ached, and my headache threatened to split my skull in two. My fight-or-flight instinct didn't kick in; it was as if my entire nervous system had shut down. If I had felt threatened, there was nothing I could do; there were too many of them to fight by myself, even with my father's powers.

I stretched my hands out, and my fingers ached, allowing blood to go back into the tips. I had ripped a nail, which I bit off before it tore into my flesh.

River finished serving a customer and approached. He still had a few days' worth of stubble lining his jaw, and his amber-brown-colored eyes smiled when he saw me. He would forever stay twenty-two years old until my father released him, but knowing my father, that would never happen. And since he could burst into a ball of raging flames, I wondered whether he sensed any powers.

"Can you feel any of my father's power coursing through your veins?" I asked, nibbling on the torn nail.

His brows furrowed, yanking my finger out of my mouth. "Not that I can feel, but then again, I wouldn't know what it feels like."

I tried thinking about the times he did burst into flames so that I could describe it to him, and I came up with a blank. "What if you thought about bursting into flames?"

His brows furrowed further, making them almost one long eyebrow. I almost laughed. But when he realized I was serious, he relaxed, rounding his shoulders and closed his eyes.

"I don't know if this will work," he said, opening one eye and closing it again. He hummed as I assumed he channeled my father. Nothing. There were no angry flames or even a tiny spark. I was about to comment when he glowed; a light blue hue surrounded his body, reminding me of an aura. I reached out to touch it when it disappeared, and he opened his eyes. "Nope. Nothing."

I lowered my hand and said, "You glowed. So, whatever you were thinking about needs to happen again, but only with more intensity."

Someone caught his attention, demanding an ale.

"Duty calls," he said with a smirk.

I sighed wearily, silently hoping he could channel his powers soonest, but in case he couldn't, we needed another plan. River needed his memories returned and to be healthy or the first demon who approached would destroy him.

I yawned as fatigue seeped into my chilled bones. Even though the sun was out, I sensed it was late evening back home already. My stomach grumbled, and I wished for a hot meal to warm me, then some sleep. Glancing at River serving another monster-patron, I hoped his room had another bed I could sleep on. I wasn't afraid of this hotel, but that didn't mean I wanted to sleep in my own room; I welcomed his company.

"Have you eaten anything?" River asked, pulling me out of my thoughts.

"Do they have proper food or must I drink the red sludge?"

He chuckled, shaking his head. "There's normal food that everyone eats. The vital fluid they drink is like an appetizer followed by sandwiches or main meals. They still eat like normal humans."

"Thank goodness, because I really wasn't looking forward to sipping on *that* kind of red tonight." I smiled, and it reached my eyes. "What time do you get off?"

He glanced at the clock on the wall, and it was ten at night. "Midnight."

I could sit here for two more hours and wait for him. It gave me time to eat and gather my thoughts about what we could do if we needed help. "Can I order a burger and chips?"

Chapter Six

The burger and chips were the best I'd ever eaten. Ever. The bun was soft; the meat was tasty, and the cheese and tomato were bursting with flavor. To say it impressed me was an understatement and especially good for a place in the middle of nowhere.

"I'm glad you enjoyed it," River said, licking his fingers. He had joined me for dinner once the bar area had quietened down.

"Does the bar close at twelve or does your shift end at twelve?" I asked, wiping sauce from my mouth as I hummed to the music playing softly through the speakers. The guitar riff playing reminded me of someone and when he started singing, I knew who it was. I loved his music; especially *Edge of Desire*.

"The bar closes at twelve and opens again at twelve."

"Jeez, so twelve-hour shifts every day?"

"Yep, or I help Henry out at reception, but luckily, it's not always busy."

"There are no televisions or radios here. What do you do when it's quiet?"

"I read," he said, jerking his chin at a book under the bar counter.

I smiled. "Do tourists book the hotel or do the residents?"

"Only the residents."

"Why? They have homes here?" I finished my cold drink and sat back in the chair. It confused me why the hotel was here, in Antarctica—where there was nothing but ice, and no tourists.

River wiped his mouth and threw the paper napkin on the plate. He stood up and poured a green cold drink into two glasses, handing me one. He sat down again, scooting his chair closer to mine.

"I haven't been able to figure it out yet," he said near my face so that only I heard. "But there is something going on here, and whatever it is, I suspect nobody wants the news to get out."

"Have you explored the hotel yet?"

"I've walked around, but I'm unable to enter most places. So, I've stopped trying to go where I'm not allowed."

I stared into his light brown eyes, then at his lips. He was so close to me, all I had to do was lean forward and kiss him like I had done so many times before. I blinked and leaned back into the chair the moment *Edge of Desire* started playing.

My chest squeezed as happy memories of us flashed before me; we were dancing barefoot outside in the puddles. His arms were over my shoulders, my arms were around his waist, with my head against his chest. A light drizzle left our skin and clothing damp. While we danced to *Edge of Desire*, he sang; his deep baritone vibrated throughout my body, leaving goosebumps in its wake. The world could be on fire, and we wouldn't care. We were the only two people who mattered in that glorious moment. Everything had slowed down for us, and I never wanted it to end.

Then, when it was time to go inside, we peeled our wet clothing off and dried by the fire... a fire that burned brightly, leaving its orange, red, and yellow reflections against our skin, warming our naked flesh. The memory dissolved as quickly as it materialized and replaced with a gut-punching sadness; I was the only one who remembered. Then again, I was also the only one who remembered the breakup.

River picked up our empty plates and took them to the back, unbeknown to him, the deep feelings I still had for him were threatening to burst out of their seams. And a thought came to mind that perhaps if his memories never returned, could he fall in love with me again? The thought caught me off guard. Did I want us to be together again? Another thought I didn't know the answer to.

Quickly, I wiped the rogue tear from my cheek before he returned and smiled when he sat back down. Hope filled his smiling eyes, and I wanted to wrap my arms around his neck and kiss him tenderly. But we were no longer a couple... we were only friends; a friend I had to help before I lost him to this world forever.

"I think it's fine to close the bar and go," River said, stifling a yawn. "I take it you have no reservation here?" He asked with a smile and a naughty glint in his eye.

"No, I was hoping your room had a couch I could sleep on."

"No couch, but there is something better," he said, wiggling his eyebrows.

River locked the doors leading into the bar area while we exited out back through the kitchen. We entered a small foyer near a set of service elevators and, to the left, double doors that led to the main reception. Above the doors was a sign that read *'Nightmare Hill'* and above the elevator doors was another sign reading *'Fallen Home'*.

"Charming," I said, pointing at the signs.

"They're all over the place," he said, pressing the button with an arrow pointing up.

I opened my mouth to say something quirky in response when the doors opened with a sinister ping. A deep red light bathed the interior of the elevator, reminding me of the Underworld.

River entered first and pressed a button on the panel. He glanced at me, waving me inside. "It won't swallow us," he said jokingly.

"Hah, that's what you say now," I answered, slowly stepping inside. "For all I know, this leads down into tunnels where one gets lost and never seen again."

"You watch too many movies." He chuckled, pressing the button to close the doors.

Once the doors shut, the red light flickered to a gentle white, allowing me to see more of the inside, and the elevator moved upward. On instinct, my eyes darted to the top of the doors, where the numbers moved swiftly; all I saw were glowing odd red numbers. I glanced at the side panel and there were only oddly numbered floors and not ordered correctly, either. It went from 1 to 15 to 37 to 51 and upward. A coldness swept through my body when I saw the number River had pressed.

As if sensing my fear, River started, "It's not 666," he said with a smile.

"No, but it's exactly half." I said sarcastically, pointing at the panel.

"I know some people think that odd numbers have bad omens attached to them, but not here."

"How can you be so sure?"

"I've witnessed nothing—"

"Yet. You've witnessed nothing… yet."

River pursed his lips for a moment and closed his eyes. When he opened his eyes, he visibly relaxed. "No, nothing has happened yet. Apart from their daily ritual, there has been nothing suspicious. Nothing evil. And nothing sinister."

He fell silent as we both watched the numbers flick from one to the next. Although I knew there weren't over three hundred floors, it took a few minutes to reach the top.

"And who am I to complain? I arrived here with no money, no memory, yet they still offered me the penthouse suite and gave me a job." He shrugged nonchalantly. "They have given me so much and asked for nothing in return. They accepted me without judgement. The least I could do was show them respect."

I sighed audibly. He was right. I had to think about this objectively. We classified the Underworld as Hell, and my father was Lord of the Underworld, and his father was most likely the Devil everybody feared. Normally, this information didn't bother me, yet it did now because it directly affected me; I was in a hotel in the middle of an icy nowhere and they filled it with monsters who didn't want supernaturals near them, yet that's exactly what they were. I was both good and evil; evil on my father's side and good on my mother's side; this should not bother me, yet... today it did.

A sharp pain started at my temples.

The elevator dinged as it stopped on a floor. The doors opened into a large foyer with marble floors and gold trimmings along elegant lines on the walls, framing intricate patterns. Blinking in bright numbers at me, 333, almost taunting me.

"Come on," River said, exiting the elevator. "Let's make you comfortable."

I stepped out of the cool elevator and into a warm foyer with the smell of cinnamon wafting in the air, reminding me of pancakes on a rainy Sunday. Cool air caressed my neck, sending waves of goosebumps spreading across my body. Another distant memory flashed before my eyes of Mom and Mason making pancakes on one of those rare occasions when Mom visited us. The memory was comforting and unnerving since I hadn't thought of that in forever.

"This way," River said, pulling me out of my thoughts. He waved me over as he crossed the threshold and into another room.

I followed him into the living area, and it felt like I had stepped into an eighties nightmare; all beige wallpaper, a fluffy white carpet, pastel blue ceiling with white blotches making it look like clouds, strangely shaped lamps that changed color, a frilly burnt orange-colored sofa and one blue floral sofa that matched the swag-draped curtains. I rolled my eyes.

"Who is the decorator?"

"It was like this when I moved in."

"It's like an eighties horror movie," I said, giggling. "Do you know who lived here before you arrived?" I asked, picking up an oddly shaped ashtray, turning it over in my hands and almost dropping the paper weight since I hadn't seen a smoker in years. Carefully, I placed the item back on the side table and followed River into the terribly styled beige, yellow, with splashes of red kitchen. I shuddered.

"I've asked questions before, but none have said much, and in the last three weeks I've lived here, nothing has happened, so I'm grateful."

"So, no poltergeists throwing chairs at you, or Babadook opening your closet while you sleep, or a demon trying to possess you?" I asked with a smirk. It sounded better in my head and now when I said it out loud, I sounded ridiculous.

"Haha, no, none of the above. This suite is spook free."

"Good to know." I entered the kitchen to see what he was up to.

He reached for something in the pantry and grabbed an original golden sponge cake Twinkie. "You want?"

"Where did you get that?" I asked, reaching for the delicacy.

"No idea. All I know is every Monday when I come home, they stocked my fridge and pantry with food and treats. They washed my laundry, ironed, and put everything back in my closet, and the place is clean. I'm certainly not complaining."

"These remind me of birthday parties," I said, opening the evil cream filled cake and enjoyed a bite, savoring the sweet, creamy taste. I couldn't remember the last time I had one of these.

"One thing you must never say here is Happy Birthday," River said seriously, almost paling.

"Why?"

"To these people singing Happy Birthday is equivalent to saying a spell, and the result is the person ages, unable to reverse time." The confusion on my face must've said a lot because he continued speaking. "You know how in the song we repeat the sentences three times each?" I nodded. "Well, it's like a spell witches cast, which is repeated three times, and we say these words three times. The song locks the person whose birthday it is in that age, until next year when they're a year older. No medical advancements or med-bed can reverse this spell."

I stared wide eyed at River, not believing what I heard. "Are you yanking my chain?" I said with my mouth full of Twinkie.

"No, I'm serious. Nobody has aged in this village since they arrived here."

"So... you're saying there's no Happy Birthday songs? No celebrations? No cake?"

"Nope."

I couldn't think of a clever retort, so thought it best to keep quiet. I glanced at the Twinkie in my hand. "Are the supplies dropped off monthly?" I asked, changing the subject, and in between mouthfuls. "I mean, you're out in the middle of Antarctica where there's no airstrip or harbor."

"Again, I don't ask questions. Things just happen. I mean, some people bake bread and catch any animal around these parts while others enjoy luxuries that are produced," he said, holding up his half-eaten Twinkie. "It's like there are two different types of people living here, those stuck in the eighteen-hundreds while the rest aren't." He shrugged and shoved the rest of the Twinkie into his big mouth. "I don't know about you, but I need to sleep." He licked the cream off his index finger. "There's a room you can use with its own ensuite bathroom, so you don't have to worry about sharing with me." He grinned. "Come, let me show you." He waved over his shoulder as he disappeared into the lounge.

I followed River through his penthouse, enjoying the delicacy as if it was the first time tasting it. We entered a long hallway with only two rooms across from each other.

"This one is mine," he said, pointing left. "You can stay here." He entered the room on the right and switched on the light, illuminating the room in a soft blue hue.

"Wow, okay, it's very… blue." The walls were blue, the bedding, the light, the curtains, and even the ensuite bathroom. "I can't remember the last time I saw a different color bathtub that wasn't white." I vaguely remembered the one apartment Mason and I had lived in which had an olive-green colored bathtub; it was terribly retro.

"It takes some getting used to, but it's a place to clean yourself and a safe place to sleep. How long will you be staying here?"

I stared at him, wondering whether he thought I was just here for a night and then I'd be gone tomorrow without him. "I'm here to fetch you, River, and then we're going back home."

He blinked like he didn't understand what I'd said. "You want to take me to a place I don't remember. I don't know if I can do that. I have a job here and surrounded by people who care about me, even though they are strange."

The silence stretched between us.

When cold air brushed lightly against my neck, I shuddered and glanced up at the air vent. The blue bathroom light flickered off and on, pulling my attention toward the blue mat on the floor. I exhaled and could see my breath in front of me. My eyes moved upward where a decaying woman laid in the bath flickered to life. I blinked, and she was gone.

"Did you see that?" I asked, pointing at the spot where I'd seen her.

"What?" River asked, stepping closer. "I see nothing."

"There was a woman in the bath," I said, still pointing. "She was in the bathtub with one side of her face smashed in." I pointed to parts of my face to emphasize my meaning. The parts of her face I could see had smudged makeup like she'd been crying, and the right-hand side of her head had a hole, as if struck by a hammer or an equally deadly object. Whatever had happened to her happened here.

"I can't see it." River squinted at the vacant space.

"She isn't there now," I said, chewing on my bottom lip. "I have a direct connection to the dead... or rather, to souls." I could push souls out of bodies, but this was the first time I'd seen visions of someone who had died violently.

"I've never felt another presence here before," he said, waving his hand inside the tub. "Since I work with your father, do I have something similar?"

"No, not really," I said. "But you did see the professor's soul three weeks ago. Your gift is turning into a raging fire skeleton."

"I don't know what to do now." He glanced my way with a worrying look. "I'm not scared. Are you? Do you think you can sleep here tonight, or do you want to bunk with me?"

"I'm not scared. I just don't want to be pestered all evening. Let me first see what's in your bathroom." I didn't wait for him to show me and I headed directly for his room; which was red. Like my room and bathroom was blue, his was a deep maroon. When I flicked on the bathroom light, no tortured soul materialized.

"Well?" he asked behind me. "Do you see anything?"

"Nope, nothing here... so far."

"Then you stay in this room, and I'll take the blue room."

"You're not afraid that woman would bother you?"

"I've been here for three weeks, and nothing has happened to me. I'll be fine."

I yawned and nodded. "Thanks," I said, glancing around the bedroom. "It should be fine." But in the pit of my stomach, I knew it would be a sleepless night.

Chapter Seven

The rising and falling of my bed soothed me as I slowly
awoke from my nightmarish slumber. The visions of the
bludgeoned women plagued my dreams. Her decaying flesh
and septic wounds pulsed with pus. While her vacant stare
bore holes into my soul as if she knew who I was yet wasn't
afraid, and every time she reached out to touch me, I woke
up feeling the burn of her caress.

Fingers brushed hair off my face, tickling my cheek. I
smiled absentmindedly and scratched my face. This dream
was lovely, and I didn't want to wake from it; I laid on a
beach with a warm breeze caressing my skin, leaving goosebumps in its wake.

"Morning," River said.

My eyes shot open, and I quickly lifted myself off his
warm chest, wiping drool from my mouth. I shivered from
the sudden loss of heat as my cheeks warmed.

"Why are you here?" I asked, feeling slightly violated.
We hadn't slept in the same bed in so long, yet it felt so right

to be this close to him. I yearned to touch his chest again but fought not to.

He smiled kindly and sat up. "During the night, you called out to me, asking me to sleep beside you. You said you had nightmares and didn't want to sleep alone."

I wiped crusty sleep from my eyes, which only made them burn. The maroon duvet cover slipped off my body and my arms pebbled. My heart raced and instead of saying something, I laid on my back and stared up at the yellow-stained ceiling.

"What can I get you for breakfast?" he asked gently, and the bed moved. "How about some coffee?" Material rustled, and I shut my eyes tightly, hoping River hadn't been naked beside me. "Or some scrambled eggs and bacon?"

I sat up as he pulled on a shirt. He was wearing the satin sleep shorts I'd given him for our first anniversary. It had yellow duckies against a black background.

"Some coffee for now would be great," I said weakly, hating that I still had strong feelings for him. If only he'd been more human, like he was now, over a year ago, then none of this would've happened. We could've been happily in love and playing house, ignoring the world... ignoring my father... and it would just be us.

"Come join me in the kitchen," River said, smiling. It was one of those smiles that tugged at my heartstrings. A smile filled with so much warmth it filled the room, making me smile with him. But it was his penetrating eyes that struck me; a fleeting glance that held so much without saying a thing. A look that meant all or nothing.

I glanced away, breaking the connection, and forgetting about the awkward feeling of waking up beside him. "Sure," I said, pulling the duvet off me, and looking forward to a nice cup of coffee.

River worked the kitchen like a pro, and he filled the Kermit mug I held in my hands with the best coffee I'd ever tasted; which was apparently made of roasted beans from Africa.

The smell of bacon and scrambled eggs assaulted my olfactory senses, making me salivate, and my tummy grumbled in hungry anticipation.

River dished up for us and sat beside me at the counter with his matching mug; both mugs had pictures of Kermit the Frog on.

We enjoyed our breakfast in silence. It relieved me the eighties styled kitchen no longer hurt my eyes; the retro colors seemed to soften the longer I sat in the kitchen.

In my peripheral vision, I watched River eat. He was the same guy, yet different. He still ate his bacon with his hands while forking scrambled eggs into his mouth. Today he parted his hair on the other side, the way he always used to part it when we were together.

"We have to see if someone can help with your memory," I blurted, while chewing. "I mean," I swallowed, "we can go back to the Underworld and find someone to help us. But we don't know who sent you here in the first place or why, and they may still be there waiting for us. Something might happen if we return, and I can't help but think that maybe the answer to our question lies here."

River scooped up the last of the egg, chewed it, and swallowed. He finished his coffee and turned in his chair to look me in the eye, as if searching for something.

After what felt like hours of staring at each other, he finally spoke. "I don't remember what happened before three weeks ago, but there's a familiarity about you that tells me I can trust you. And whoever had hurt your father and banished me here is trying to tell either you or your father something. And yes, I agree with you. There is something about this place that maybe we'll find the answers to what had happened."

Hope blossomed in my chest, and the weight of the unanswered questions lifted slightly off my shoulders.

"Good. Now, who can we speak with?"

The elevator screamed to a stop on the ground floor, opening to the foyer. Henry stood behind the counter, assisting a couple checking in. He raised both eyebrows when we approached and waited patiently behind the couple. The couple took their key and headed for the elevator.

"What can I help you with?" Henry said, folding his muscular arms across his chest. He had rolled his shirt up to his biceps, revealing the tattoos on his forearms reading "MAKE ME", which still irked me somehow.

"Is there anyone we could speak with regarding River's memory?" I asked, eager to get going.

River nodded. "I remember when I first arrived, and you offered to take me in, you mentioned someone I could speak with who could help me, but I've been so busy lately with work it completely slipped my mind."

Henry nodded and leaned against the counter. "I could direct you, but you haven't ventured outside of this hotel since your arrival. You need to be careful," he said to River, then he looked at me. "And you," he said, narrowing his eyes, "have no place being here. Whatever you are, I sense something." He slowly stood straight, towering over me.

I swallowed hard, not wanting to give him any details about who I was.

"We'll be fine," River said, drawing Henry's attention. "We are aware of the strange happenings in your village, and we'll never say a word, but if there is someone I could see who could help me—"

"You don't know the half of it, my son, but I won't stop you from leaving. In fact, I encourage it and wanted you to see her when you arrived."

"I know. I don't know why I didn't though," River said, frowning. "Thank you." River proffered a hand.

Henry took River's hand in both of his and held him for a few seconds. Tiny electrical sparks pricked at my skin. Henry let River go and scribbled something on a piece of paper.

"I'll take over your shift in the bar. There aren't many checking in this afternoon so it should be fine. Just be back before midnight."

"Why?" I asked.

Henry's eyes flittered to mine. I didn't know this man but sensed a familiarity whether it was the color of his eyes, the shape of his face, or just him, but I sensed something, too.

"The White Devil will make its way through the town again," he said seriously.

Chapter Eight

Henry was cryptic and creepy all at once, but at least we could read his handwriting on the piece of paper. We had to see Faye, who produced most of the various potions that helped the townsfolk having headaches, heartburn, and other ailments.

We exited the hotel, and I could hear something like static electricity in the distance. "Can you hear that?"

"What?" River said, obviously not hearing the same thing as me.

'Scout?' A voice called. 'Are you there?'

'Jake?' I thought back. 'Is that you?'

'Yes.'

'What took you so long?' I'd reached out to him after my father had left me here almost a day ago, but unlike other spirit animals who would immediately appear beside their owner, mine had to fly to me.

'Snow, so much snow!' If Jake had teeth, they would chatter now.

'Be careful, these townsfolk hunt crows.' I warned, crossing the street after River who had entered a shop with no signage. I glanced around, realizing none of the shops had signage, and I wondered how he knew which was which.

"How do you know where to go?" I asked, catching up to him. "And do they charge?" I remember asking Neville this question, and he didn't know what money was.

"They don't use money here but provide for the love of it. Everyone just provides. It's just that simple... and different. Nobody pays rent or for water and electricity. Everything is free. It took me the first couple of days after I had arrived to understand who was in which shop," he said with his hand on the door handle. "And Faye is in this one." He opened the door, and a bell chimed.

'I see you,' Jake said, sounding closer. I glanced up in time to see a black object move toward me. With only a second to react, I caught the flying icicle in time to ensure his sharp beak didn't stab me in the heart.

"Hey buddy," I said, rubbing his wet head and body. "I've missed you." Jake snuggled into my hand and slowly the ice melted off his feathers. I dusted the snow off his head and smiled when his beady black eyes met mine.

"Who is that?" River asked with his hand still holding the open door. "They don't like crows here," he whispered. "If I were you, I'd hide him now." His expression sent a chill down my spine.

"Climb into my jacket," I said, unzipping, and Jake snuggled his damp body against my shirt, wetting me. I wouldn't allow anything bad to happen to my spirit animal and would gladly get wet and cold for him. "Where are the others?" I whispered.

'I knew this would be dangerous and told them to hang back until I need them.'

"Good thinking," I continued in hushed tones. River stared at me like I was nuts. "What?"

"Who is he?" he asked again.

"Oh, sorry, this is Jake, my spirit animal."

"Spirit animal?" He shrugged, shaking his head. "I know about demons, vampires, werewolves, and leprechauns, but not spirit animals." It saddened me that River didn't remember spirit animals. He was the one who had told me about spirit animals when I met him, and he had his own.

"For some supernaturals like my father and myself, we don't shift or change into anything, but we get a spirit animal. And mine are Jake and his fellow crows."

"Cool," River said, smiling. "I like that idea." He fell silent for a moment, then added, "Do I have a spirit animal?"

"Yes," I said, averting my eyes. "Her name is Luna, and she's a Mexican mutt."

"Do you know where she is?"

I shook my head. "No, I don't. She was with you when you disappeared."

The silence stretched between us.

"I wish I remembered how to channel that side of me." He furrowed his brows. "I wish I remembered you and Luna. I hope she's okay," he said dismally.

"Me, too. But that's why we're here. Let's go inside and find out if she can help you, and then we see about finding Luna." I jerked my chin at the shop and River entered first.

I followed closely behind River, holding Jake close to my body, and glanced at the various bottles displayed on shelves. No two bottles were the same, yet they were all just as intricately shaped. Some bottles had hints of pink or blue or green near the top, and inside each bottle were different colors matching the color of the glass. The labels I could read as we walked past were of things I'd never heard before; Ritual Energy Enhancer, Anointing Liquid, Cleansing Liquid, Plant Charging Liquid, Magical Floor Wash, Magical Healing Spray, Scrying Mix, Bathing Brew, Calming Potion, Easy Tea Blessing, Moon Water, Love Potion, etc., to name a few.

One part that stood out was there were no prices on any of the magical bottles. It amazed me that anyone who lived here could approach Faye and ask for something and not have to pay a cent. If only the real world worked that way; to offer your services for free and not expect anything in return; what a blessing. If only it happened everywhere; a world where we didn't have to worry about money for food or rent. That we only focused on what we truly wanted to do. It would be a world where there were more kind, creative people than bossy managers and corporate suits. It would be a world where there was more love than hate, more good than bad, and way less crime. I wished that world would happen and soon.

"River," someone with a delicate voice said beyond the shadows. I squinted in that direction but saw only a counter and dark wallpaper. Then the shadow moved, and a fair skinned woman came into the light. It was strange how she blended with the patterned wallpaper behind her; her dress was of a similar pattern. She was about a head shorter than me and wore layers of clothing without her looking like a bag-lady. Her hair was more salt than pepper, and she had fine lines near her mouth and on the sides of her emerald-green-colored eyes.

"I'm glad you've found the time to stop by," she said,

closing the gap. "I've been waiting for you to visit me since your arrival." She reached for River's hands, squeezing them, then she approached me. "And you must be Scout. I've been waiting for you, too." She smiled kindly.

"Yes, ah," River stammered. "You know our names."

"I do," Faye said, not divulging any more information.

"Can I ask why you didn't approach me sooner?" River asked.

"You weren't ready to hear what I have to say, son," she said kindly.

River nodded, then thumbed at me. "She's come to take me back—"

"Home," Faye said, holding my cold hands with her warm hands. Her smile reaching her eyes. "She's here to help you heal, as am I," she said mysteriously.

"Thank you," River said.

Faye patted his shoulder like a mother would a child. "Now, the most important thing for you to do now is open your mind when the time is right. You need to allow your memories to flow through you." She turned and headed toward the back. "Come on," she said, waving over her shoulder for us to join her.

Jake moved his now warm body against my stomach and nestled himself comfortably. I continued cupping him with my left arm to ensure he didn't fall out from under my jacket.

We followed Faye into a tiny room at the back of her store. The room was big enough for two people and only had a washbasin, so for the three of us standing there felt terribly squished. My arms brushed against Faye's and River's, with poor Jake squashed against my stomach.

Faye leaned into our little triangle, her eyes darting

between River and me. "What I'm about to tell you now, you must never repeat," she whispered. We nodded our heads. "You need to find Mother Nature within these worlds," she pointed at our feet, "she's the only one who can help you."

Chapter Nine

We went back to the hotel suite to pack a bag with refreshments. Henry confirmed he would take over River's shift at the bar, giving him time to find what he needed. Regarding Mother Nature, apparently, she had been hiding here in Antarctica for decades, avoiding my uncle, Seth. If I had to guess the reason, it was because she had an affair with my father, and they had two sons. And Seth wanted to hurt Mother Nature or punish her for leaving him.

"I find it weird," I started as I rubbed my temples. "Growing up as a kid, we were always told that Mother Nature wasn't real." I shrugged. Like most people, we were told she was just a myth, a face that explained nature, or a figment of our imaginations.

"Do you think your father would know more?" River asked, packing us each a backpack. It reminded me of the first time we'd met, and he had helped me on the quest my father had sent me on. Except instead of a backpack, River had pulled the sandwiches and cool drinks out of nowhere.

He had said he could teleport the food from where he'd made them back in the Underworld.

"He might," I said, not looking him in the eye. "But doubtful he could help us now. He's investigating who is responsible for what happened to him and you." I trusted the old River but wasn't sure whether I could share my thoughts regarding Mother Nature and Seth, and my demon-half-brothers, with this new River.

"But like Faye said, Mother Nature has been in hiding for centuries and nobody knows whether she's truly in the tunnels. It's only a rumor."

"That means we might go down there for nothing, and nobody can help you." I sounded as deflated as I felt.

'Or you might find something better,' Jake whispered in my head. After all these years, it still unnerved me how I could hear a bird talk inside my head.

"You're right, Jake."

"What did he say?"

"That even if we don't find Mother Nature, maybe by going down there, we'll discover something that may help."

River sighed wearily, as if life itself had taken its toll on him. "I just want to remember."

"Me too," I smiled weakly and blinked. I turned to look away so he couldn't see the tears and went to the red bathroom to freshen up. "I'll be out in a second," I yelled from the doorjamb, closing the door behind me.

'Have you noticed River has aged?' Jake asked in my head.

'Huh? What do you mean?'

'Exactly that, the three weeks he's been living here, he already has fine lines around his eyes. When he was still that ball of angry flames, he looked twenty-something. But now...' Jake left his words hanging.

'He isn't feeling well.'

Jake cawed loud enough for me to hear behind the bathroom door. I hurriedly finished and as I opened the bathroom door, a cold breeze licked my neck. It was so arctic it seemed to slice through my clothing and sink into my bones. The feeling of numbness increased until I stopped and turned around.

I came face to face with the woman from the bathtub; her transparent, bludgeoned face hovered close to me. Her surviving eye blinked at me. If she were alive, she might have been beautiful; with flowing, long auburn hair, sharp features, and a lovely curvy body. Unfortunately, someone took a hammer or something equally heavy to her skull.

She opened her mouth to say something, but nothing came out. When she realized she was mute, her expression changed, unnerving me. Unfortunately, not all souls could communicate verbally with the living.

"What? What are you trying to tell me?" I said, stepping backward.

Her lips moved erratically as she tried telling me something, but all I heard were bubbles popping. Based on her animated expression and how she was trying to communicate with me, it was important. I shrugged and shook my head.

"I can't hear you. Can you write it down?" I glanced around the red room for a piece of paper and a pen and found them in the bedside table drawer. "Here." I handed her the items.

She stared at the items and shook her head, lifting her arms in surrender, and continued mouthing her story slowly; over-pronouncing each word. I wasn't good at lip reading but I got three words; 'don't trust him', before she looked at something behind me and dissolved into nothing.

"Ready?" River said behind me, making me jump. "Are you okay?" he asked, placing a hand on my shoulder.

I turned around and out of his grasp. "Yeah, um, sure. Let's go."

"What are you doing with that?" he asked, pointing at the notepad and pen.

I wasn't sure whether the ghost was referring to River or someone else. If I told him what she said, would he think it was him and then I was in danger? But why? It made no sense. She was wrong; she had to be wrong. I knew River and trusted him. It had to be someone else. Yet I didn't want to tell him what had just happened.

"I wanted to make notes before I forgot it, but now I've already forgotten what I wanted to remember," I said sheepishly, handing him the items. "It doesn't matter." I thought it best not to say anything until I knew what she was trying to say.

"Ready?" he asked again.

"Yes, let's go," I said with excitement. "Let's get your memory back."

With our backpacks on, we exited the elevators on the ground floor and traversed past the bar area. The doors were closed, but I heard them chant the end part of their late lunch ritual. '...*And with our lips, we'll drink from your vein. Our souls forever yours.*' I shuddered, remembering yesterday how they drank their red liquid while in their natural creature-vampire form.

"Does everyone do that thing here?" I whispered, pointing at the bar door.

"No, some do it at home or wherever they are," River

said. "I think they like doing it collectively, as if it makes the words more powerful."

"Makes sense," I said, still unsure about these creatures. I had more questions about them but doubted River could answer, so I thought it best to leave it alone for now and focus on our adventure and him healing.

We traversed through the town and headed for the pond. Faye had whispered that there was a tunnel near the pond; we were the only ones in her shop, yet she felt the need to be cryptic. I didn't understand this town. They hated supernaturals, yet they were themselves, with Faye reminding me of a clairvoyant since she already knew our names. She had said it would lead us to a place where we could find someone who knew where Mother Nature was or direct us to Mother Nature herself. It all felt hearsay to me.

We passed Faye's shop, then a bakery, then a fish shop. The delicious smell of warm buns quickly squashed the stench of smelly fish.

Someone ran past us frantically yelling at the shop owners for help.

"Hey, what's wrong?" River caught the man by his elbow, stopping him.

"It's Neville," the man said. "He's dead." His eyes widened in terror. "We've had no one expire before."

"How can that be?" I asked.

"Nobody is supposed to die here, that's why," the man said sarcastically. "It's the reason we do the daily ritual. That's why we drink the blood of our gods. That's why we are strong." He raised his fists in praise, then turned his cold, dark gaze on me and sniffed. "That's why we stay away from your kind."

I stepped closer to River, then remembered he could do

nothing for us if this guy unzipped his human skin and lunged at us.

River stood tall and glowered down at the man. "Don't be rude, Roy," he said, poking his index finger into Roy's chest. "And apologize to the lady."

"Bah!" Roy mumbled, turning on his heels and continued yelling down the street. "Neville is dead! Neville is dead! He's by the pond. He's by the pond."

Those in their shops exited and headed in the pond's direction. We followed closely behind but were careful not to get caught up in the crowd of people.

"Come here," River said, pulling me to one side. We followed along the wooden fence circling the pond and stopped on the far side, away from where the crowd had gathered. Now that I was so close to the pond could I see only one half of it was frozen.

I squinted in the distance at Neville's crumpled body on the red soaked snow. They had picked parts of his face, but I saw no vultures or other birds of prey, except crows sitting on the far side of the pond... waiting.

Jake felt my uneasiness. I knew those crows didn't belong to us but I was still worried about them. They cawed and the middle crow took flight, flapping its large black wings, and the rest followed. They flew overhead, cawing as they went.

The crowd hissed at the birds while some crouched, raising their claw-like-hands to protect their faces. Their performance was unnecessary. The crows did nothing to them.

Jake moved uncomfortably in my arm under my jacket. *'I don't like this,'* he thought inside my head.

'Me neither,' I thought back. Then I turned to River and said, "Where to now?"

River glanced around and jerked his chin in the blue pole's direction. "There," he said, holding out his hand.

I glanced at his hand like I had done so many times before and slipped my smaller hand into his without thinking. There was nothing to it, even though any kind of touch was intimate for me. But I knew now wasn't the time to think about our relationship or what had gone wrong between us. We needed to find Mother Nature and get River healthy again.

We ran along the outside of the fence, as if we were going back toward town, then the path curved around the pond to the opposite side of the pond. The crowd in the distance looked like dark ink blotches, and it relieved me they paid us no attention.

"I wonder what happened to Neville," I said nervously. The last time I saw him was when we were at the bar, and River and I were chatting in the corner. I couldn't remember seeing him any other time.

"Whatever it was, has just stirred something," River said gravely. "I may not have lived with them long, but I don't think they will stop until they find the culprit."

The wind cut through my jacket and bit into my flesh, making me shiver. It was either that or River's words unsettled me. "Has anything like this happened before?"

"Not since I arrived," he said, reaching for the blue wooden pole. "But last week someone came into the hotel with an open wound on their arm, blaming the crows and everybody stormed the streets stoning any bird that flew nearby. No bird neared, as if they expected the outrage. But this, one of them being murdered, will cause havoc."

I didn't like the sound of this. It was one thing stopping someone from getting hurt, it's another having a lynch mob out for vengeance. I was glad to be here where there was little threat.

River stepped forward, reaching for the blue pole, and waved in front of it. Something popped and whirred, then a device extended out of the pole. This reminded me of a retinal scanner, but instead of showing one's face, River pressed his thumb into it. The device whirred again, moving out of the way, and the floor opened near his feet.

River removed the fake rubber thumb we received from Faye, which was an imprint of her thumb, and pocketed it in case we needed it somewhere else.

"I wonder why only some residents know about this," I said, staring down into the dark hole.

"Maybe Faye is an elder," River said, crouching to get a better look.

I nodded. It made sense. When I had first arrived, Neville had said the elders were here first, and they kept the town safe. Perhaps not divulging this information about the tunnels below kept them safe. The last thing anyone wanted was to have an influx of unwanted attention.

"Ladies first," River said, holding out his hand for me to take. With his help, I stepped down into the dark abyss of an underground world we knew nothing about.

Chapter Ten

The dank tunnel ran deep underground, so deep it felt like I was in a gold mine. Water dripped down both sides of the stone wall, then dissolved into the soil at our feet. Small pebbles littered the uneven ground as we traversed our way through the dark shaft.

River walked beside me, our flashlights shining dimly up ahead. "Faye said we need to look—" River left his words hanging as we approached a section of the tunnel that had more pebbles against the sides than anywhere else. "For this," he continued, crouching.

I kneeled beside him, grabbing pebbles, and placing them behind us. Once all the pebbles were on one side, we started digging with hand trowels.

"I'm not seeing anything," I said, throwing sand over my shoulder. "Faye said there'd be a button somewhere."

"She didn't know how deep we needed to dig," River said, digging without looking at me. Faye had said nobody used this side entrance much, therefore she didn't know what condition we would find it in. Sweat peppered his forehead and dripped down the sides of his face. He wiped it away with the back of his hand, smearing mud on his forehead.

"Here," I said, wiping the mud off for him.

"Thanks," he said, staring at me and for a split second, bright flames flickered inside his brown eyes. "What?" he asked.

"Your eyes, I saw flames—"

"Hey, you!" someone yelled behind me. I glanced in their direction, and two men started running toward us holding torches.

"Hurry!" I yelled, digging faster.

River struck something hard, and we froze. He reached inside the hole and yanked on the leaver. The ground shuddered beneath us as the two men stopped running and held onto the beams for support. The wall in front of us moved to one side. Darkness greeted us, and once my eyes adjusted, I saw a slide. I groaned inwardly; against my better judgement, I climbed onto the slide. I was about to slide down a tunnel I knew nothing about and hoped it wouldn't be my last breath. River climbed in behind me, snaking his arm around my middle with a leg on either side of me. He punched the button against the wall with his other hand, and the door shifted closed, locking once more.

"Go!" River yelled, and we slid down the slide together.

———

It relieved me we didn't crash into a wall, or worse, into a pit of snakes. Instead, the slide moved gently up and down, reminding me of an amusement park for toddlers. Eventually, it straightened out gently and came to a stop where we could stand up without falling over from the momentum.

The area where we stopped, though, was something else entirely, and I struggled with words to describe it; cavernous, otherworldly, intense. And definitely unbelievable. A Mammoth Cave.

I took my phone out of my bag and snapped a few shots, quickly tucking it back in. I didn't want to be caught taking photos for fear of retribution.

"Wow," River said beside me, his jaw dropping open. I reached for him and pushed his mouth closed.

"Close your mouth, you're catching flies," I said jokingly.

"Look at this place," he said, reaching for my hand like he did so many times before. And like before, I didn't pull away and casually slipped my hand inside his. And like always, it felt so right touching him and it was comforting to be here with him even though his intentions were that of friendship.

Focus. I reprimanded myself. Sometimes I got lost in my own thoughts. Apart from the anger I had toward my father and what he did to River. River and I had our problems within our relationship, too. I had always craved his physical touch, always needed extra reassurance from him, used humor to mask my pain and laughter to mask my hurt. Perhaps it was because he was my first boyfriend that I'd fallen so hard for him. And that's why touching River like this, now, only made me want him more. The distance I'd put between us this year had hurt, but it also had helped me to recover; out of sight out of mind. But touching him now like this, it sent too many memories and emotions I'd buried out in the open.

'The heart wants what the heart wants,' Jake whispered inside my head and moved within my jacket.

'Yeah,' I groaned. *'And right now, it's bleeding emotions.*

Besides, they bruised his head, and he needs time. And nothing is guaranteed.'

Jake didn't respond, instead he nibbled on the finger holding him.

River and I walked hand-in-hand toward a pink rose bush and admired the sweet-smelling plant. We joked and laughed and enjoyed the moment. On our right-hand side was a glistening blue pond, up ahead stood rows of corn, and above us a light as bright as the sun.

"I don't understand," I said, sounding dumbstruck. "How can all this grow underground and with that light?" I shrugged. "It's wonderful that plants grow here."

"There are worlds within your world," said a female voice in surround sound. Her words bounced off the sides of the walls without hurting our ears, yet I felt the vibrations within my chest.

I clutched Jake closer to my chest, my thumb rubbing his chest; his heart was racing, too.

"Hello?" River said, glancing around. "We're here to see Mother Nature... or someone who knows where she is."

"Who are you?" The female voice asked, and again her words bounced against the walls and into my body. The same had to be happening to River too because he clutched his chest with his free hand.

"We're River and Scout," River said.

A warm wind blew into us from behind. "And what do we have here?" The wind opened my jacket wide enough for Jake to stick his head out.

"Please don't hurt him," I begged, feeling overly protective of my spirit animal.

"Come this way," the voice said, her words vibrating within me once more. The warm wind blew against our backs, egging us onto the path through a vast, luscious garden.

We traversed through the vegetable garden and then a flower garden, where there were bees buzzing, stridulating insects, and a frog croaking. Hummingbirds and butterflies fluttered past. The longer we walked, the louder the stream became until we eventually came across a small rocky waterfall and pond. Beside the pond stood a weeping willow, its long branches greeting us in the gentle breeze.

I unzipped my jacket, airing it out. Being underground was much warmer than above surface and I hoped Jake could fly around without being hunted. Jake hopped onto my shoulder, craning his neck to look behind him. I turned to see what he was staring at and grabbed River's arm. He turned to see what we were staring at and froze.

A dark-haired woman wearing a white sundress sauntered toward us. She almost seemed to walk in slow motion as the wind blew her hair slightly backward and her dress moved elegantly against her curvy body.

River's jaw dropped again, and I did everything I could not to close his mouth; if he wanted to embarrass himself, so be it.

The woman stood before us with a contagious smile, and I fought hard not to smile back. She radiated enchanting beauty, and I wanted to touch her or bottle her essence to keep on a day when I felt depressed. Then I could breathe in her essence and feel whole once more. She was happiness on steroids.

I blinked, snapping myself out of the trance I'd found myself in, and River coughed into his hand, his cheeks flushed.

"Welcome," she said, her eyes twinkling with humor.

"We haven't had company in a while. What can I do for you?"

River and I spoke at the same time. It was a mixture of words that hurt my ears. The woman raised her hands, shushing us. She pointed at River.

"I arrived in Antarctica three weeks ago with no memory of who I am or how I got there," River started. "Yesterday this woman," he thumbed at me, "arrives and claims to know me. She has said some outrageous things that I don't know if I can believe her. I mean," he glanced at me, "I want to believe her, but I just don't know. You know." He shrugged. "And I want to remember who I am."

I wanted to open my mouth and tell him I told the truth, that I was here to help, but if he was unsure of me, then we needed someone objective who could assist. It hurt to hear him say that he didn't know if he could trust me; I didn't lie. But I could only hope that whoever this person was, she could guide us... him, in the right direction. I had to remember that he was the one in need of urgent help. Even though I wanted him to come home with me—and to be mine once more—it was up to him. When his memory returned, he could decide whether he still wanted me as much as I wanted him. But he needed to remember first.

My shoulders sagged in defeat, and I glanced at her obediently and with hope. The woman reached out and placed a warm, calm hand on my shoulder. The heat from her touch seared through my body and I did everything I could not to allow my knees to buckle.

"Scout means you no harm, River. Her words are true and..." she stared into my eyes, through me, and into my soul. I wanted to pull my jacket on again to cover myself but doubtful it would help; she had a way about her that could strip you naked without touching you.

Jake flapped his wings and cawed, but eventually settled down again, rubbing his head against my cheek. I petted him, then scratched under his chin.

"Jake is a wonderful spirit animal," she said with a kind smile. "He'll always protect you." When she let go of my shoulder, I felt the immediate loss of her warmth. I shivered and pulled on my jacket. Jake flapped his wings, and when I was ready, he settled on my shoulder again.

The woman stood before River and said nothing. She was his height, a whole head taller than me, and just stared at him for what felt like hours.

My legs were aching, and I was about to sit when she spoke. "River, there is a way to gain your memory back, but it will be dangerous."

Chapter Eleven

Why did everything have to be dangerous? Could life not be a smooth ride filled with happiness and a deep sense of calm? What the Lady of the Garden had told River almost knocked me on my bum. We were in a world not like our own, it was far from the Underworld, and we didn't know what to expect. Yet somehow, we had to gain entrance into another Secret Garden, but before doing that, we had to fight dragons.

Dragons...

I was not fond of dragons. Not that I fought them often, or at all, but I had heard how others had and almost lost their lives. And not forgetting that we couldn't trust dragons. Their kind was one of the trickiest shifters out there. Don't get me started on fae. They were the worst, but we wouldn't be battling them today. I hoped.

But... it wasn't only dragons we had to fight. Before we reached the Secret Garden, we needed to maneuver through a maze to get what River needed to restore his memory... the Heart of a Dragon.

We left the Lady of the Garden in search of the entrance to the maze to retrieve the Heart of a Dragon. Jake snuggled into my neck, comforting me, as an uneasiness started spreading within my bones. I dreaded the fact that once again, we'd be entering a maze. The last time we did this, we almost didn't make it out alive.

"When you get your memory back," I started, "you'll remember the first time we entered a maze."

River glanced at me out of the corner of his eyes, and his mouth curved upward. "Yeah?"

"Yeah," I said, smiling. "It was scary though, but you helped me through it."

"Cool." He was silent for a moment, then added, "I hope what the Lady of the Garden said was true, that I'll gain all my memory and my health." He coughed, wiping his mouth with a material napkin. He pocketed the napkin so quickly, but I had already seen the spot of blood.

"I hope she's right," I said, feeling hopeful and scared. "Then we can get out of here." I wanted nothing more than to have River healthy and us back home.

"Do you know how old I am?" he asked, pushing a tree branch out of his way. We were heading for the far corner of the cavernous area. Apparently, somewhere between rocks was another leaver that opened to a world filled with mazes.

"If I'm not mistaken, you're about forty-five in human years, but you look twenty-something," I said, staring at his profile. Jake was right. River was aging; he never had fine lines near his eyes, yet now there were one or two and a few strands of silver hair on the sides of his head.

"And you mentioned that I've been working with your father for over twenty years?" He glanced at me, frowning.

"Yeah," I said, facing forward. I didn't want the guilt or shame because of what my father had done to him.

"And he collects souls?" He sounded angry, and I didn't blame him. I hated what they did. That's one reason I left River, ignored my father, and started working with Mom.

"Yep," I said, "and you help my father in retrieving those souls." My reply was slightly higher in pitch with full-bodied anger.

"To save my mother?"

"That's what you told me when I first met you."

"Is she still alive?" His tone was gentler and with less venom.

"No," I said, calming down and glancing at him once again. "She passed away soon after you started working with my dad."

River stopped walking, forcing me to stop too. I waited for his response. Perhaps I'd finally see some flames of anger in his eyes. Something. But he did nothing but stare into the distance. His expression did change and as I waited for the wrath of his rage, my heart thudded in my chest.

What came next surprised me. River wiped the tears from his eyes and tried to smile. "It was my fault, wasn't it?"

I nodded once. "Yeah, nobody should make any deal with anyone from the Underworld, regardless of their rank. And there's always fine print you'll never read and only once they have your soul locked in place will they reveal the true cost of what you have done."

"Has your father tied my soul to his?"

I nodded once again. "He keeps the link to your soul safe—"

"And the others?" he asked and continued walking.

"The others," I shrugged, "I don't know. My father doesn't share much of that with me, but I know the link to your soul is safe and sound." I hoped. That's what Father had said. That it was safe.

This conversation could've gone differently. We were both getting angry over something out of our control, but we realized that and instead of yelling at each other, we spoke elegantly and with compassion. Sometimes I allowed my emotions to dictate my words but as I matured, I thought before I spoke. Well, sometimes.

We traversed the rest of the way in comfortable silence and, much like the first quest we had gone on, this place did not disappoint. Our short hike through the various gardens was uneventful. I sighed with relief but knew what was ahead would be challenging.

We reached the corner wall of rocks and searched for the leaver the Lady of the Garden had mentioned and River found it right at the bottom. He pulled the leaver down and cogs moved behind the wall of rocks. Then, something shifted, and the wall of rocks moved to the right, revealing an opening.

"Are you ready?"

———

Once the rocky door opened and we walked through it shut closed immediately, as if managed by a sensor. The next world we entered was unlike the one we had just left, which was bright, flowery, and alive, while this one was dark and walled. Thorny vines wrapped themselves around the tall dark gray walls and near the top blossomed red flowers. It was pretty in a strange, twisted way.

The high gray walls seemed to disappear into the dark sky, and unlike the previous world that seemed like a large cave, this one seemed open and limitless. Above us twinkled stars, or it was a black ceiling with lights; it was difficult to decipher whether we were out in the open or inside a massive dome-like-structure.

Although these under-worlds reminded me of the Underworld, they felt different, like they had built each world for a specific purpose. Whereas demons had created the Underworld for demons where they imprisoned souls. These hidden worlds beneath the surface were worlds within worlds. They were magical.

A breeze blew between the high walls, creating a sinister whistle that made all the hairs on my body stand up. At the moment, we were in a safe space, but I didn't know how much longer we could stand here without being harmed.

Not wanting to stay in one place like prey, I pushed River toward the only way I saw out. "Let's go there," I said, heading for the tight gap between two walls. As I passed between the two sections, I glanced up; the wall on the left was so high I couldn't see where it ended, but the wall on the right was twice my length with moss growing over the edges.

"What if we bump into a creature the Lady of the Garden warned us about?"

"We'll manage as and when that happens," I said, not sounding convincing. I didn't know the answer to his question and hoped the creatures coming after us took little effort to destroy. Rounding my shoulders, I clicked my neck. I had powers of my own and could manage if River wasn't able to fight back... I hoped.

"This way," River pointed at another opening to our left, but as we neared, we realized it was a wall; the illusion of a thin opening was just the thick, dark mortar between the bricks.

I glanced around, squinting. "There," I said, pointing at

another section of the enclosure that seemed like another opening, but when I got there and touched the wall, it was the same as the other side. "Now what?" I surveyed the small area in search of a way out. "Where did we enter from?" I turned around and approached the part we had just walked through, and it had walled up. "I was sure we came through here."

"The walls keep moving," River said, walking along the oddly shaped enclosure we now found ourselves in with his hand on the wall, feeling for an opening. His hand brushed against the moss and vines and he stopped and backtracked. "Here," he said, walking into and through the wall.

"What? Wait?" I ran to the spot where he had just been, my hands feeling the way, and just as he had slipped through between two walls that stood at odd angles to each other, I did too. "This place is freaky," I said, almost bumping into the back of him. "Why are you standing still?" I asked, stepping around him and froze.

Standing in front of us was a chunky naked man with fiery red hair and beard. He was a little person, but his demeanor was that of a giant. His grin stretched his face as he winked at me.

"'Allo gorgeous," he said. His voice was gruff, like he smoked a pack of cigarettes a day. "Want to play with me?" he asked and started doing that hip pelvis maneuver men liked to perform for women when bragging about the tricks they can do with their penis. This man was making his go side to side with that slapping sound each time it hit his legs.

"Um, thanks for the invitation, but I must politely decline," I said, as unthreatening as possible.

The man stood taller and glowered. His nostrils flared and his fiery red hair moved. I'd met a man like this one once before on a case with Mom and Ralph. A relative of his, Stheno, who was ferocious and had killed more men than her sisters, Medusa and Euryale, combined. Stheno would lure men into her room, where she had her way with them, before killing them. And if I had to guess, this man with slithering red snakes for hair was a cousin of Jedediah.

"Here," I said, handing River a pair of sunglasses I retrieved from my backpack.

"What are these for?" he asked.

"If you wish to remain flesh and bone, put them on or this gorgon will turn you into stone." I slipped my sunglasses on, and the man's eyebrows scrunched together and he pursed his lips.

"How dare you?" He snarled. "I was looking forward to playing with a pair of stone figurines." And then he lunged for River, his slithering hair snapping their venomous jaws, trying to bite him. I reacted on instinct and lunged for the gorgon. We connected, my hands landing on his damp, naked, hairy chest while his hair hissed at me. He reached for my shoulders, but I pushed him backward before he could touch me, but instead of him going backward, his soul flew out of his body and, with my momentum, I pushed his body to the floor like a crumpled rag doll. I side stepped, avoiding falling on top of him.

The gorgons' soul hovered above us, clearly dumbstruck by what I'd just done to him.

"Holy crap," River said beside me, and I heard him smile without turning to see if he was. "What did you do to his body?"

"Well," I said, shrugging, "I'm the daughter of the Lord of the Underworld, and manipulator of souls. With these hands," I fisted my hands and opened them again, "I can push souls out of bodies." I rounded my shoulders and my large black wings extended and flapped, lifting me off the ground.

"And you, gorgon," I pointed at the soul, "don't belong here." I needed to get rid of him before he realized all he had to do was float back into his body. The last thing we needed was a gorgon following us around and trying to turn us into stone.

I whistled, and the Ferryman appeared with a light mist enveloping him. He glanced around, his eyes wide, then he saw the soul and smiled. He nodded curtly in my direction, scooped up the soul, locking him on his boat, and the pair floated off into the distance, then they faded away in a trail of mist.

River rubbed his eyes. "Did I just see that? Did that just happen? Wow, I can't believe I just saw some guy in a boat floating in the air with a second face at the back of his head and scoop up a soul. Oh, my gods," River rambled. "I can't believe I saw that."

I stared at River and smiled. This was the first time he had seen something like that. Previously, he would ask what I was doing if I had been communicating with a soul or pushing their soul out of their bodies. Perhaps his sight was infrequent. I would ask Father when I saw him.

"Come," I said, levitating back onto the ground and my wings disappeared. "Let's go." As the words escaped my mouth, a high wall shifted into place separating River and me. "No, this isn't happening again." I grabbed River's sleeve and pulled him closer to me. He lost his footing and crashed into me. I couldn't hold both of us up and we landed on the ground with a loud thud, my head hitting the ground hard.

"Are you okay?" River said, getting off me as quickly as he had fallen on top of me. "Here," he said, holding out his hand for me to take.

"Ow!" I moaned, rubbing the back of my head. "That

hurt." I grabbed his hand, and he pulled me up gently. I swayed for a moment, River still holding onto me, ensuring I kept my balance, and once I felt okay to stand on my own, I stepped away from him. "Thanks," I said, my cheeks heating.

"Why did you pull me like that?" he asked, pulling his sleeve straight.

"The last maze we were in, we got separated and I panicked now. I didn't want that happening again."

"Oh," he said, nodding. "When did that happen?"

"It was a few years ago," I said, thinking of the quest my father had tricked me into doing. "I was sixteen when my father sent me on my quest to become what I am today. It's almost like an initiation thing I had to go through in order for my father and his siblings to accept me as part of the Underworld family. And you were the one who helped me survive it."

River smiled. "Cool," he said nonchalantly. "I'm glad I could help."

Jake cawed, pulling our attention to our surroundings. The wall that almost separated us moved again, halving the space we were in.

"That way," River said, pointing at a wide opening. We bolted for the space between two high walls and crossed in time, the walls slamming into each other with a solid clunk. I swallowed hard, imagining one of us being squashed between the heavy slabs of rock, and grateful at the same time that we were still in one piece.

"This place is baffling," River said, reaching for a brick that stuck out. When he realized it was loose, he pulled it out completely, revealing an opening.

I stepped closer and scraped the goo oozing out,

bringing it near my nose. "It smells like sweet cocoa." I brought it close to my mouth and stuck out my tongue.

"Don't taste it," River said, pulling my hand away from my mouth. "What if it's poison?"

I immediately wiped the goo on an open piece of brick until my finger was clean. I watched the goo move and squirm, latching onto the brick, then it bubbled until a sizeable chunk of the brick was gone. "Jeez, that was close." I wiped my finger on my pants until I was sure the stuff was off my skin. "Let's try there."

In the far corner stood two bright green hedges with purple roses, and between them a hole big enough for us to crawl through. The closer I got to the hedges; only then did I realize that the roses also had a white trim on the edges of the petals.

"These are beautiful," I said, reaching out to touch them, but thought better of it. It seemed anything beautiful in this maze became deadly. It also reminded me of Alice falling down the rabbit hole and nothing in this place was as it seemed. I glanced at River and knew it would be worth it in the end.

"Let's go through without touching the hedges. One never knows." River went onto his hands and knees first and crawled through. "It's safe on this side," he called. "Come through."

I straightened the backpack and went down on my haunches, crawled, and was careful not to touch the sides of the hedges. Once through, River grabbed my arm, pulling me up.

"Mind your step," he said, pointing at the gaping hole that stretched from one side to the other. "It feels as though each room has a booby trap or some sort of test." He pointed at the hole.

I peered inside the deep black hole but saw no light anywhere. The darkness moved, and I squinted, wondering whether what I saw was real or if my eyes were playing tricks on me. The black inkiness moved again, and I bolted upright and against the hedge.

"What did you see?" River asked, peering over the edge. "I see nothing." As River stepped away from the edge, something large flew out of the hole and up into the dark sky. "What was that?"

"I don't know, but I don't want to hang around and wait for it to introduce itself." I glanced at the hole in the ground and realized it wasn't that wide and I could jump over it, but I needed someone on the other side to grab me if I didn't make it. "You jump to the other side first," I said, pointing. "And that looks like an exit in the corner."

River glanced up and then at me, shrugging. "Sure, I can make it, but I don't see an exit there."

"We can't go back now, so there has to be a way out there somewhere."

"Okay, let's do this." River exhaled audibly and sucked in a deep breath. He pushed his foot against the root of the hedge that was sticking out of the ground, crouched lower, then kicked off running. He sprinted the three steps and leaped into the air. Something flickered around his body like his aura had sparked, then disappeared quickly when he landed on the other side. He made long jump look so simple.

"Now catch me if you think I won't make it," I yelled. My heart thundered inside my chest, sweat peppered my forehead, and goosebumps spread across my skin. I pressed my heel against the other hedge root and readied for my sprint. I was not a fast runner at school and an even worse long jumper, and my legs were not that long. Exhaling a deep breath, I pushed against the root. My four steps were as fast as I could go, and when I vaulted into the air, the hole seemed to yawn and stretch. For a moment, it looked like my outstretched legs were going to make it. I was going to land on the ground near River, but the hole moved.

River's panicked face told me everything I needed to know. While his outstretched arms tried to reach mine, I felt my body sink quickly as the air beneath me sucked me down. I tried swimming in the air to reach River, but I was no bird. Wings. I had wings. I couldn't believe I'd forgotten about them. My wings appeared and flapped behind me, but the darkness wrapped its inky tendrils around my ankles and pulled me down.

River reached out for me and seemed to follow me down, our fingers almost touching. A yellow flame sparked at his fingertip. My wings continued flapping. The hole swallowing me. Everything was happening so fast, yet in slow motion. And with one final flap of my wings, I grabbed River's hand.

Chapter Twelve

I understood how Alice felt when she fell, not feeling the weight of gravity. We fell and fell and fell and the surrounding darkness moved yet became nothing. I wanted to stop my flailing arms, my wings flapping and my legs kicking, because it wasn't helping. No matter what I tried, I kept falling through the dark abyss. I wanted to get off this weightless ride and stop falling, and that's what I did. I stopped moving. The instance I stopped moving, my feet touched a shiny flat surface.

I stood still with my arms wide open, trying to keep my balance, but it wasn't necessary. When I realized I was no longer falling, I stood straight and sighed, smiling to myself.

River realized what I had done and did the same. The moment he stopped moving, he stood beside me. He too kept his arms wide open until he regained his balance, then he stood tall with a nervous smile on his face. "That was weird," he said.

"I know," I replied, pushing hair out of my face. A breeze cut through my clothing, and I shivered. The wind changed direction, and it felt as though the floor beneath us shifted, sending us to one side. Then slowly, the inky darkness lightened. The room turned shades of white, gray, and black, with staircases materializing and going in all directions.

"What is going on?" I asked, not believing my eyes. There were stairs above us, to the side, against the walls, below us, next to us, all around us. There were rooms and archways leading to various passages and balconies. Everything around us was confusing, strange, and in different directions.

"Relativity," River said.

"Huh?"

"The Dutch artist MC Escher printed a lithograph in 1953 featuring staircases where normal laws of gravity don't apply." He pointed at a staircase above us. "This reminds me of that picture."

"I've never heard of him, but I'll take your word for it." I glanced up at the staircases and swallowed hard. Tiny butterflies fluttered inside my stomach, thinking about walking on the upside-down staircases. "How do we get out of here?"

"One of these staircases must get us out of here."

I groaned inwardly. I didn't like this, but I followed River anyway. We approached the closest flight of stairs that curved along the wall. I grabbed the cream-colored marble banister and slowly traversed up the steps. We climbed about fifteen steps and came to a short platform that split into two staircases. River took the stairs on the left, and these stairs led to another platform, a set of staircases which we had to choose from, and then another platform and stairs. When we finally reached the first balcony, we peeked over the edge.

"Whoa," I said, grabbing hold of the balustrade before I fell over. We were upside down. I glanced at my feet firmly planted on the floor, expecting them to lift off. My hair didn't float in the air, nor did it feel like I was about to fall over. "This is so weird." I let go of the balustrade and raised my arms. It felt normal, like I was standing on a hotel balcony.

"I know," River said, grinning. He was enjoying this. "Let's go there." He pointed at another staircase leading to a door with wrought iron hinges and handle. "No other door looks like that one, it must be the way out."

I glanced at the staircases and how they branched in different directions. My vision tunneled and my head spun. I white-knuckled the balustrade and quickly glanced at River before I lost my balance.

"Come," he said, running up the next flight of stairs. "Let's go here." He sounded like a little boy in a candy store.

I reluctantly followed him, each step leaving me feeling queasier than the last. I dared not glance over the railing at the ground below for fear of the floor breathing, opening its mouth, and me falling over and inside the depths of darkness.

"What if someone flicks a switch, gravity changes and we fall?" I asked as the staircase moved beneath me, almost swallowing me whole. It took everything I could not to look. My stomach did a flip-flop, and I gripped the hand railing, white-knuckling it.

River chuckled. "Are you okay?"

"No!" I yelled as nausea took hold.

River continued laughing as he traversed up the stairs. He pushed the door with the wrought iron hinges and handle open and stepped back. "Wow," he said, glancing over his shoulder at me. "Hurry, you don't want to miss this." And he stepped through.

"Wait," I groaned, quickening my step. I forced myself to take each step without looking behind me and finally reached the door, stepping over the threshold.

Chapter Thirteen

We arrived at a high platform that had a bird's-eye view of the giant walled maze. It was the centre of the maze and the Town Square. There were people hustling and bustling about, going from one shop and into another while some were eating at various restaurants.

"Wow," River said beside me. "This place looks magical yet familiar," the lines between his eyes deepened, "like a town somewhere in Europe."

"Uh huh," I said, my eyes bouncing all over the busy place. Swallowing hard, I licked dry lips as I searched for a sign letting us know what this place was. I squinted and pointed at a plaque on fired clay bricks that reminded me of Rome. "This place is Agartha," I said, confused.

River followed my finger and nodded. "I know that name," he said, deep in thought.

"Me too, but I can't recall how or where I heard it from."

"It's that inner Earth conspiracy stuff." River nodded,

agreeing with himself. "Yes, that's where I saw it. Inner Earth."

"How can it be real?" I asked, not quite believing in this esoteric stuff. "Why were we never taught this in school if it is real?"

"There are always reasons they keep things from us. Well, we were in an underground tunnel, then we went through a large garden, a massive maze and now we're at the center of it all. So, either we're both hallucinating, or this place is real." River glanced over the edge. "Look," he pointed, "There's a rope ladder against the wall."

"At least we have a way down," I grumbled, not looking forward to climbing down the rope ladder—it was not my favorite way to scale down a wall. No matter what I did, I always broke a nail, scraped myself and bled, or some other injury. "But before we go. We have a vantage point, so let's see where we need to go."

The Lady in the Garden provided little instructions. She had told us we needed to fight dragons, get the Heart of a Dragon, and gain entrance into a Secret Garden. We had already maneuvered through the maze, House of Relativity, and now we were back in the center of the maze. Now all we had to do was find the place where we had to fight dragons.

From my bird's-eye view, I got a good look at the town within the center of the maze. On the outskirts of the Town Square was the never-ending maze. I glanced up at the still night sky and although it felt open, I couldn't help but think some large glass structure covered us. What I thought were stars were lights. A part of the maze sounded as it shifted and moved, blocking one section off.

"We need to go there," River said, pointing at the water feature. In the center of the Town Square sparkled a large water fountain. "Do you think it's made of genuine gold?"

"It looks like it." The female statue held a jug and water poured out of it and into the fountain reservoir below. Standing behind the woman was a dragon in a protective stance. People cupped the crystal blue water that flowed freely from the jug and drank from it, while others threw golden coins into the fountain and made a wish or two. "It looks like the dragon is protecting her," I said, wishing we were closer for a better look.

"Either that or it wants to eat her."

I rolled my eyes. Sometimes men always went for the negative outlook on life. "We need to get closer."

"Look there," River said, pointing.

Someone played classical music near a drinking fountain on the far side of the Town Square. The water floated horizontally in the air, making squiggly waves that changed with the music. With each change in frequency and vibration, the water changed shape; the squiggly wavelength either became high—the amplitude—or low and spread out depending on the frequency of the music being played. It was a marvel to witness, reminding me I knew nothing about my surroundings and science, and I couldn't wait to get home to try this out myself.

"That's pretty cool," River said, hypnotized by the change in shape of the water. He blinked, snapping out of the trance. "Let's go," he said, shuddering. He glanced nervously around and I followed his line of sight. In the distance, something flapped its large wings.

"It looks like the same thing that flew out of that hole causing us to fall like Alice."

"It looks like a giant mosquito."

I squinted at the slender, elongated body and piercing

mouthparts. When it opened its veiny wings and flapped, it hovered above one of the high walls. I imagined how it could easily snatch someone with its mouth and drain the person of their blood. None of the residents seemed bothered by the giant winged creature.

"Let's get down before it sees us," I said, pushing River toward the edge. "I'd hate to go through all this only to be consumed by a large bloodsucker."

"I think I'd rather take my chances with a vampire than that thing."

"Exactly."

"Ladies first," River said, helping me down. I grabbed hold of the rope, turned around, carefully placed my foot on a step, and slowly descended the rope ladder. River came in after me at a much quicker speed. I just touched the ground in time and got out of the way, avoiding River's fast descent.

We stood staring at everyone walking past us, and none noticed us. I wasn't complaining. The last thing we needed was unwanted attention. Silently, we traversed through the sea of moving bodies and, without bumping into anyone; we headed for the water feature.

I glanced at the various shops we passed, and it felt like a busy city center. One shop sold handmade clothing, another shop owner sold hats, and there was even a chocolatier. The people looked like normal humans with normal colored hair, and they wore normal clothing; jeans, t-shirts, dresses, shorts. Everything about this Town Square was *normal*, except it was an underground world at the center of a maze. The air smelled like it did on surface and although I wasn't sure about the stars, warmth caressed my face as if the sun was out.

I glanced around to see where all the people lived and

there were only shops nearby, but I found multiple paths leading in and out of the town square. They probably slept in places I couldn't see from here. Then I tried to see if there was something different about the place, but I found nothing out of the ordinary except one thing. The water fountain.

We reached the large marble fountain with statues covered in gold. The water flowing from the woman's jug was the clearest blue I'd ever seen. I cupped some water and drank the liquid; it was cool, refreshing, and I felt it move down my throat and into my stomach.

"I can't believe you did that," River scolded. "There could be parasites in the water." He shook his head. "This place shouldn't be taken lightly," he warned. "We don't know what's going on here or if we can even consume anything."

"It was fine." I wiped my hands dry on my clothing. "And I'm fine." He was right, though. For a moment, I'd forgotten where we were. For a fleeting moment, I'd forgotten why we were here.

We were quiet for a moment as we stared at the water fountain. The fresh water in the fountain was inviting. If we weren't on a quest, I could imagine us jumping inside and splashing around like a couple of naughty kids. The marble structure was solid; I couldn't find any lines where pieces joined. It was as if they had carved the entire fountain out of one large block of marble.

"Let's look for something," I said, changing the subject. If the water was poisonous, then I'd die soon. There was no point in moping about it. We had a job to do. "We're here, let's look for clues."

River walked around the fountain while I walked around the other side. We passed each other, still looking for something. Anything. The large golden statue of the female and dragon seemed to watch us circle them. Their strategically placed unseeing, unmoving eyes constantly watching us.

When I met up with River at the same spot from where we started, he shrugged. "I see nothing. It looks perfectly made. No lines, no joins, no buttons, or markers. Nothing. Not even a scratch."

We passed each other again and walked around once more. I traced my finger along the smooth, cold edge, feeling the water spray against my face as the water flowed from the jug into the water below. I touched the jug, and that too was cold and smooth.

Looking up at the golden statue of the woman and dragon, their eyes on me. Their forms were large and imposing at such close proximity. Again, I saw no lines or rough edges. Their bright golden color sparkled in the light that came from everywhere. I glanced up, and a light glowed above the Town Square. It wasn't the sun I was used to; it was something that seemed to illuminate the space above us. The entire area was strange, and that perhaps the stars I saw at the start of the maze were tiny lights and that the maze was inside an enormous dome of sorts.

I exhaled a frustrated breath and continued walking around the large fountain. I stopped and stared; bolted against the bottom of the fountain was a plague that read; *Agartha and Her Dragon's Heart.*

As calm as ever, I hurried to where River waited and tugged on his arm. He silently followed me to the spot where I stopped and pointed.

"You found it." His smile widened.

"Yeah," I said, elated. "Now what?"

River crouched and started poking at the plague. When

he struck the third bolt, it clanged loose. He unscrewed that bolt, then the rest, and placed them carefully on the floor. Then slowly removed the plaque to reveal a lever.

River glanced up at me as he reached for the lever. I wanted to tell him not to, to wait, but I'd lost my voice. The light above us flickered. And River pulled.

Chapter Fourteen

Everything that happened next materialized in slow motion. River pulled the lever. The townsfolk froze. The light above us flickered again. I held my breath. The lever moved, the water stopped flowing from the jug, and the water inside the fountain drained in the floor beneath. Once all the water had cleared from the bottom of the fountain, the floor shifted down, forming a staircase.

I leaned over the side of the fountain to see, but there was nothing but thick darkness. "Not again," I grumbled to myself. I was always up for an adventure, but going down into an unknown darkness was not something I looked forward to. Which was counterintuitive since my father was Lord of the Underworld; I should be used to the darkness and seeing monsters and demons, yet whenever I needed to do something dangerous that involved darkness, I retreated just a little. To take my mind off the blackness below, I glanced around.

"It's like they're being controlled," I said, pointing at the people frozen mid-step.

River shook his head. "Nothing makes sense." He combed his fingers through his hair and I noted more strands of gray had appeared. "Maybe they're not even human."

"Hm, maybe."

River stood beside me, then climbed over the side and stepped onto the first step. "Are you ready to take the next steps?" he asked, pleased with himself.

"Yeah," I said, "I'm coming." I climbed over and stood beside him.

River removed his flashlight from his backpack, switched it on, and descended the stairs that spiraled against the wall. I wondered whether this was an old well that was converted into a water fountain that someone could switch off to get down there. What exactly was down there was yet to be seen.

I removed my flashlight and turned it on, but the darkness was so thick I could only illuminate about thirty centimeters in front of me and all I saw was more darkness or the black shiny stairs we were traversing down on.

Slowly, we descended into the bowels of the dark fountain where the air was cooler and smelled like wet cement. I shivered, dreading going any farther, but I had to.

"What do you think is down here?" I whispered, and instead of River answering, a wind kicked up, blowing my hair out of my face.

"Maybe it's the dragon," River finally answered. "Whatever it is, has to help me." He sounded more confident about his quest than he did when we first started.

When another breeze blew my hair out of my face, I froze and turned toward the darkness. Squinting into the abyss, I shone my flashlight in the direction the wind had come from and reached for River, but he was too quick and disappeared from my line of sight and into the inky blackness.

"River?" I whispered. I swallowed hard when he didn't answer, and another wind blew into my face. "Crap," I mumbled to myself and ran down the stairs, bumping into the back of him. "Why did you stop?" I grumbled, holding onto his arms to keep myself from falling over.

Another wind blew against me, warmer this time, and I slowly turned to look in that direction and a pair of crystal white eyes blinked at me. Large eyes. Eyes that reminded me of mother-of-pearl, or liquid silk. I swallowed hard and blinked slowly. With a shaky hand, I moved my flashlight in its direction. Then those enormous eyes moved up and up, and then its black body materialized as the creature stood.

"I don't like this," I said, gripping River's arms like my life depended on it. I giggled. My life did depend on him. We needed each other, and I wished his memory returned so that he could turn into his angry skeleton of flames and save us.

"What do we do?" he asked. His voice breaking.

"I don't know," I whispered, still holding onto him with one hand.

We stared back at the creature, waiting for something to happen, but nothing did. The creature glared at us with its crystal white eyes that sparkled as the light struck it.

I didn't know what to do but knew I had to do something. After a moment, I let go of River and stepped forward. River reached out to pull me back, but I swatted him away.

"Hi," I said, the flashlight shaking in my hand. "We're looking for the entrance—"

"To Mother Nature's Garden?" The creature said, standing taller. The light from above touched it, revealing more of the creature; its shiny black scales with purple and blue hues, barbed tail, large batwings, and an even bigger toothy mouth that definitely breathed fire.

"Um, yes, we need her help—"

"She's no longer here," the creature said, licking its lips. "There's no one here who can help you."

"We're also looking for the Dragon's Heart. Do you know where it is?"

The dragon laughed, but it sounded more like a displeased grunt. It coughed and plumes of smoke emitted out of its mouth. It moved its enormous claw and pointed a glass-like-talon fingernail at the spot where I assumed its heart was.

"This is the only place where you can get a Dragon's Heart."

I swallowed hard and heard River swallow too. "Isn't there a better way?" I asked, not wanting to fight a dragon, and definitely didn't want to kill it. I glanced over my shoulder at River and knew we had to. The dragon was as big as a house and more dangerous than a crocodile. All the dragon had to do was open its mouth and breathe fire on us or swallow us whole.

The dragon chuckled, and the floor beneath our feet shook. Tiny stones fell from various parts of the wall, almost hitting us. A deep crack formed on the floor at our feet.

"No tiny human, there is no other way. If you're here to collect a Dragon's Heart, you're at the right place. I'm the only dragon that has what you need. Is it for him?" The dragon pointed the same glass-like-talon at River.

"Yes," I said, not wanting to take my eyes off the dragon.

The dragon nodded. "It will be a fair fight," the dragon promised. "You'll get what you deserve."

I didn't like the sound of that threat, but I also expected nothing less. Dragons were tricky, powerful, and deadly. What we needed was the element of surprise. To attack the dragon before it could attack us. I could push the gorgon's soul out of his body so the underground worlds didn't affect my powers, and if I needed to channel my father's power to defeat this dragon, I would.

My large black wings opened behind me, and flapped, tiny black feathers floated to the ground. My power coursed through my veins, strengthening me. I rounded my shoulders and more feathers floated near my face.

The dragon puffed smoke in our faces, its crystal eyes sparkling with humor. I suspected it would enjoy torturing us, then munching on our bodies and bones with its tea.

"What can I do?" River asked nervously. I glanced at him and saw flames in his eyes. When I blinked, the flames had died down.

"Nothing, just stay out of the way," I whispered and levitated higher up so that I came face to face with the dragon. "Let's dance," I said, darting for the dragon's one crystal glass eye.

The dragon barely lifted its taloned claw, slapping me out of its way. The impact sent me crashing into the wall on the far side, and I slid down to the ground with a solid oomf sound. Dazed and confused for a second, reality set in that I was fighting a dragon and I quickly climbed to my feet, readying to attack. I glanced up at the dragon, only to find it smiling at me. This was going to be tougher than I wanted.

I clicked my neck, then my knuckles, rounded my shoulders and winced. My right shoulder ached, but I quickly squashed the pain. I had no time to nurse my wounds, and besides, I would heal myself shortly. My healing took longer than most supernaturals, but much quicker than a normal human. I only had half of my father's supernatural DNA and half of my mother's, and among that concoction of supernatural, spooky DNA, I was still very human.

"Are you okay?" River asked, closing the gap.

"I'm fine," I said, raising my hand, "stay out of the way."

River held up both hands in mock surrender and stood back against the wall near the stairs. He glanced nervously at the dragon and back at me. I assumed he felt completely helpless... much like I was feeling at the moment.

I sucked in a deep breath, hiding my fear, and approached the dragon with purpose, or pretended I had a plan. I didn't know how to defeat the dragon or remove its heart, so I would fake it till I made it.

The dragon smiled knowingly. "I'll use my left claw this time. It's not as quick as my right."

I harrumphed at the remark. "You may use any claw you wish, dragon, either way your heart is mine."

"We'll see about that, little one." The dragon moved, standing taller than it already was, and the tiny bit of hope I held onto got squashed into a million tiny pieces on the floor, along with my bravery.

I sucked in a deep breath and continued approaching the dragon with the bit of gusto I still had left and flew out of the way just as its barbed tail took a swipe at me. Then I ducked as its left claw reached for me. I flew around the dragon's head, missing that tail, ducking that claw. Our little fighting dance continued; he took a swipe at me and I ducked or flew out of his way, until I was tired and sweating like a pig in the corner, trying desperately to catch my breath.

River ran to me with a bottle of water, and I finished it before he could say 'hi'.

"What are you going to do? Out dance it? Wait until it dies of boredom?" River said sarcastically. "It looks like you are playing with him. Now get out there and kill it so that I can get on with my life."

"Stuff you, I'm trying my best."

"I thought you had powers?"

"I do."

"Well, use them."

"What do you think I've been doing?"

"No idea, playing?"

I pushed the empty water bottle into his chest, and he tripped and fell, hitting his head against the wall and crashing to the ground with a loud groan.

"You didn't have to do that."

"You pissed me off," I said, then turned to the flying lizard chuckling at me. "You," I pointed an index finger at it, "what is your problem?" I saw my nail had chipped during my fighting dance with the dragon and I bit the offending piece off.

"Hahahahaha," the dragon roared with laughter. "I'm having fun. Aren't you?"

"No," I said, wiping sweat off my brow. "What powers do you yield?"

"Oh, little one, if only you knew the truth."

"Well, tell me then, because whatever you're doing with me isn't fair. I should've been able to at least draw blood by now." Glancing at the knife in my hand, I swapped the knife with my left hand and stretched out my right hand, which throbbed. I needed something to drink that had electrolytes in it to stop the cramping.

I exhaled a frustrated breath and stomped my way to the dragon like a spoiled child. Something sparkled in my peripheral vision to my right, and I glanced in that direction. I stopped dead and stared.

"You lied," I accused the deadly dragon, "your heart has been there all along." I pointed at the glass box on the far side. I approached the item but kept looking at the dragon to ensure it didn't kill me before I reached it.

The dragon roared loudly, causing more stones to fall around us, and another crack formed on the floor at my feet. I kept my balance, jumping over a crack that enlarged, and ran toward the glass box.

Heat beat against my back as a yellow and red flame lit my view of the box, but the dragon didn't aim its fire to hurt me. I placed my hands on the box, surprised by the coolness.

Wind whipped around me as the dragon moved behind me.

I heard River stand up, moaned as he stretched, and ran to stand beside me. "The dragon, Scout, the dragon!" he yelled nervously.

"What's wrong with the dragon?" I asked, finally tearing my eyes off the glass box, and turning around. I swallowed the rest of my sentence when a small fluffy dragon standing our height waddled closer to us. It had the same crystal white eyes that were still smiling at me.

"What's going on? What are you?"

"I like you two," he said, grinning. "Take my crystal heart and use it inside The Garden. If Mother Nature is still there and wishes to see you, she'll help you find what you're looking for. And you my boy," the dragon turned to River and touched his arm with a furry claw, sans any sharp-glass-like talons, "your power shines in your eyes. Just believe in yourself."

The dragon spun around and sashayed away from us, his furry bottom swaying from side to side. He was terribly cute and cuddly, and I wanted to hug him for not eating us. He pulled a black cushion out from under the darkness and into the dim light shining from above, crawled around on the cushion until he was happy he had found the best spot, reminding me of a dog on his basket, and he laid with his head on his paws, staring at us.

"Well, that was unusual," I said, turning back to the glass heart. "Let's take this and go."

Chapter Fifteen

Jake awoke from his slumber when I pulled my backpack on. He squawked and flapped and smiled lazily—or as much as a crow could smile—at me.

'What did I miss?' he asked inside my head.

'I can't believe you slept through all the action,' I chastised. *'You nap too much, lazybum.'*

'Mind your own business. I had weird dreams. Death. Murder. Oh look, I see you have the heart of a dragon. Can we go home now?'

Jake reminded me of a squirrel that was easily distracted. *'No.'* I grumbled my thought.

'Why not.'

'We first need to find Mother Nature.'

'Ah, she's been in hiding for centuries. There's no way you'll be able to find her. Unless she wants to be found.' Jake moaned in my head. If he complained any more, I might need a painkiller.

'Maybe she'll help us.' I thought, needing to be positive, for River's sake.

'Doubtful.'

'Pessimist.'

'No, I'm a realist.'

'Shh, we're here.' I scolded.

After I had placed the glass heart inside of River's backpack, we had traversed back up the stairs that curved along the wall of the fountain, pulled the lever the other way and the stairs had closed, forming the bottom of the fountain once more. Water had continued pouring out of the woman's jug, filling the fountain. The townsfolk had moved as if nothing had happened and continued ignoring us.

We didn't know which direction to go in until River had pointed out a sign that read *The Garden*, and since we had nothing to lose, we had followed the cobblestone path. It didn't take us long to reach the sign; it was a short distance from the Town Square.

"Do you think it's that simple?" River asked beside me. We stared up at the entrance to *The Garden*.

"I can't believe we didn't notice it before." I glanced down the path we had just walked down, then at the sign. It was too easy.

My eyes danced across the tall leafy-green hedge that doubled as a fence. A well-trimmed leafy archway opened into a small garden filled with colorful flowers, and surrounding the garden was another leafy hedge. I assumed this garden was only the entrance into the main garden, where we hoped we would find Mother Nature.

I stood in the archway—it smelled sweet—waiting for River, who stared at me with wide eyes. A spark flamed inside his eyes and for a fleeting moment, I thought he would burst into his flaming skeleton. But he didn't. River passed me and entered the small garden.

Jake squawked on my shoulder, digging his nails through my jacket and into my skin. "Ow," I said, pulling his talons out of me. "Be careful, would ya?" I chastised my crow again. "What's going on with you?"

"What's going on?" River asked, stopping in front of an enormous set of wooden doors carved to look like the rings of a tree.

"Nothing, just my crow going weird on me," I said to River, then turned to stare at Jake. "What do you see?"

'I don't like what's beyond those doors.'

'What do you mean? Can you fly ahead and tell me if there's danger?'

'No,' Jake thought inside my head and continued flapping his wings. He tried flying higher, but he seemed unable to go higher than the top of the archways. *'There is an invisible barrier stopping me.'*

I hurried after River, slamming my hand against the wooden door before he opened it.

"What's your problem?" he asked, sounding angrier. He gripped my hand and pried it off the door.

"Jake's getting a weird feeling. Just be careful when you open the door."

"You take orders from a bird?" he said, glancing up at Jake.

I lowered my hand, almost yanking it out of River's grasp. "What's up with you?" I asked, concerned about his reaction. When I shook his shoulder, he jerked awake and out of my touch, staring vacantly at me.

"What happened?" he asked, confused, and glanced around.

I stood in front of River and gripped his shoulders so that he looked me in the eye. "Where did you go?"

"I don't know," he shrugged, "one moment I was standing outside looking at the garden sign, the next I'm here and you're shaking my shoulders." He wiped sweat off his brow and the flames I'd seen in his eyes earlier flared to life, then winked out. I gasped when a brown strand of his hair on the top of his head turned white. "What?" he asked, looking up to see what I was staring at.

"Your hair, pieces of it is turning white."

When River glanced back down, deeper lines had formed near his eyes and mouth. I wanted to let him know what was happening, but I also didn't want to cause him any panic. Jake cawed beside me, seeing what I saw, then settled on a rosebush near us.

I lowered my hands and stepped backward, giving him space. "The sooner we find Mother Nature, the better for you, and even though we're in a hurry, take your time. We can't go rushing through doors without checking first. We don't know what's on the other side of that door."

River nodded and knocked on the door. With each knock, the door creaked open. When nothing jumped out and attacked us, he pushed the door wide open. "I don't know what happened earlier or why my hair is going white, but I agree with you. We need to find Mother Nature now. I'll watch my step, but I'll need your help. Okay?"

"Deal," I said, smiling, but it didn't reach my eyes. "Now let's see what's out there."

Jake flew over our heads and through the open door. I peeked through the opening and my mouth slackened. Entering the Garden first, I glanced up and marveled at the beautiful trees that reminded me of the rain forest, but what took my breath away were the trees that grew in circles forming a covered path. I couldn't understand how the trees could grow in perfect circular shapes with their roots sticking out from the ground on one end while the top of the trees grew into the ground on the other side, and the branches in between entwined around the tree trunk. It reminded me of those bricked moon gates I'd seen in gardens around the world. But that wasn't all, placed on the trunks were wooden steps so that anyone could climb up a tree and sit on top.

"Wow," River said beside me, "have you ever seen anything like this before?"

"No," I said, sounding dreamlike and touched the tree closest to me, ensuring it was real. "This is amazing."

Jake flew to a tree farther away, squawking as he went.

The moon-shaped-trees lined a well-used path and in between each of these trees weeping willow branches swayed. And on the ground, someone had placed uneven steppingstones. The path was more zigzag than straight, but it was still pretty.

We traversed up the zigged-zagged path, enjoying the beauty of the garden. The air smelled like rain and a fine mist rolled in from the side. Out of the corner of my left eye, I spotted something dark with large, outstretched wings, but when I glanced in that direction, it was nothing more than a hollowed out old tree trunk with shadows dancing against it. I chalked it up to the darkness, causing confusion, and hurried in front of River. I glanced behind us, at the closed door we had just walked through, and was grateful there was nothing following us.

Jake squawked louder, and I turned in time to duck before a low-lying branch decapitated me. "Jeez," I grumbled, "that would've hurt." I touched the metal blade protruding from the tree branch, and it was sharp. It wouldn't have been a big deal if it was only one blade, but the entire tree branch had hundreds of these blades sticking out. Anyone running wouldn't see this and would've met their demise.

"I thought the Garden was supposed to be all flowers

and sunshine." River lifted an old leaf covering a hole in another tree. Inside the hole, someone had tied a piece of wire to a nail. He followed the wire to another hole in another tree across the path and, if pulled taut, it could decapitate you.

"I think the important question is, who is setting these booby-traps and why?" I ducked under the wire and first tested the stone before placing my foot. If they had buried landmines, I didn't want to be the one to find out. When nothing clicked beneath my foot, I continued up the path.

"This is the strangest garden I've ever seen."

"Nothing about these underground worlds is normal," I mumbled.

We traversed up the winding path with circular trees guiding our way and kept an eye out for more traps; we found reeds covering a hole with wooden spikes sticking out of the ground. There was a muddy pool to one side I imagined was quicksand, and they strapped a huge log with a sharp point to a tree with a rope around it.

It relieved me we reached the end of the circular tree path unscathed, but the next section of the garden seemed scarier. We stood at the top of a hill and stared. The land before us was barren, like the trees had suffered a fire, and running in between the trees were small black and inky looking streams. While the sky above us was an ominous red, and the moldy path of pebbles was once white. The air was warm and sticky, and it smelled like burned wood and ash.

"I hope there are no booby traps," I said, glancing at the path behind us.

We stood on the boundary where the two different garden sections met. The differences were so stark, like day and night. I squinted in the distance but saw no end in sight.

"It reminds me of good and evil," River said, pointing at the flower garden behind us, then the burned garden we were about to enter.

I glanced at the two gardens and understood what he meant, but where one would think the flower garden was good, it wasn't; there were booby traps everywhere that would kill you if it had the chance. Then the burned forest looked evil, like there was danger at every turn, but there was probably nothing we had to worry about.

"What can you see?" I yelled to Jake, who flew up ahead.

I see nothing but barren lands. Come. I see no traps here.

Are you sure?

Yes.

Good. It relieved me he saw nothing, but we would continue to keep an eye out for anything strange.

I reached for River's hand, and he glanced at me with a kind smile. His hair had whitened some more, and his hand was cold in mine. The lines by his eyes had deepened and his skin had paled. He stepped closer and his movements were slower. I wanted to ask if he was in pain but thought against it.

I glanced away and wiped my eyes dry. I needed to be strong for him but seeing him change like this and so quickly had taken me back a bit, and I didn't want him seeing my tears. Biting my lip, I blinked vigorously until no more tears welled in my eyes. Sucking in a deep breath, we walked ahead, still holding hands.

We traversed up the dark path at a much slower pace than before. River winced with each step but said nothing. It pained me to watch him suffer, reminding me of Victor after they had used the Mask of Immortality on him. River not only lost his memory but was dying, too.

When the murky stream up ahead widened, becoming a flowing river with a deserted rowboat left ashore. I smiled as an idea popped into my head; I could row us to where we needed to go while River rested. It was better than him walking this path in pain, and me spending my energy keeping him upright.

"River, look," I said, happily dragging him behind me. "Let's go for a boat ride."

River coughed and wheezed as he hurried behind me, almost tripping over a pebble. He climbed into the boat first and I pushed the boat into the dark waters and jumped inside, careful not to get my shoes wet. I picked up the oars and started rowing. It relieved me that the water wasn't acidic and there were no crocodiles or snakes hiding beneath the watery shadows. Not that nothing was in there, but at the moment I couldn't tell.

'We're taking the boat.' I thought my message to Jake so that he knew which direction to expect us from. *'Do you see anything?'*

'There's a couple here—'

'Really? What do they say? Is Mother Nature there?'

'Let me finish my sentence. Um…' he left his word hanging, and a nervousness settled in my bones. What if we were heading into a trap? I sighed wearily. Everything about this quest had felt like a trap, but with luck we had come this far without much harm.

'What is it?' I asked carefully.

'You'll see when you get here.'

Annoyed with my spirit animal, I rowed harder, and relieved the current was strong enough to help us along quicker. We passed many burned down trees and buildings that were no longer occupied. The smell of hot ash filled the air, while the sun continued glowing yellow/red, creating an atmosphere similar to gloom at the end of a war fought long ago. I hoped the couple Jake had found could help us find Mother Nature.

My heart dropped to my feet when River slumped over. "River?" I yelled frantically. "Are you okay?" I set the oars inside the boat and reached for River. He didn't fight me as I pulled him closer. His hair now completely white, and he'd aged twenty years in five minutes. "What did they do to you?" I said, my voice croaking as the tears fell.

The stream flowed gently, taking us with it. I didn't want to let go of River in case something else happened and held him tightly against me. I cried until there was nothing left and allowed the murky water beneath us to guide us to wherever we needed to go.

'I see you,' Jake said inside my head. *'What happened to River?'*

'He's dying, Jake. River is dying. We need to find Mother Nature now.'

'You're almost here. Then we can see what needs to be done.'

The stream came to a dead end, and the boat floated onto the sandbank. Carefully, I placed River onto his side inside the boat, pulled out an emergency blanket to cover him, and climbed out. I pulled the boat farther out of the water and beside a burned tree. I tied the rope around the tree and pulled, grateful the tree didn't crumble or break apart.

Jake flew beside me as if sensing my despair. In tearful silence, I followed Jake to the place he wanted to show me, which was only a few steps away from the boat. I kept glancing over my shoulder, ensuring River was still there and the stream hadn't swept him away. I eyed the stream narrowly; it made little sense. The stream continued flowing, but it seemed to flow underneath the ground. I shook my head, trying not to worry about that now since River was my priority and silently prayed this couple could help us.

I spun around and jogged to where Jake sat. I wanted to meet the couple Jake had mentioned but when I reached them my shoulders dropped. "What's this, Jake? They can't help us," I yelled, pointing at the couple. "They can't do anything for anyone." Tears welled in my eyes again and I didn't want to fight the tears and allowed them to fall down my face.

'They're all I found,' Jake thought inside my head. His tone gentle. *"There's nothing else here,"* he said sadly.

The hope I'd been holding onto shattered onto the ground into a million pieces, and saving River became a distant memory. The way I felt now there was no way to save his life. There was no way I could get him out of here without help from someone else. Unfortunately, my wings could barely keep me up in the air, my phone didn't work here, so I couldn't phone anyone, and I couldn't allow Jake to fly out of here on his own to call for help for fear of him being hunted. And I wasn't capable of teleporting myself and River back to the Underworld; he had to be carried out of here.

A pain spread across my chest along with a deep-rooted fear. I turned in River's direction and he was still motionless inside the boat. The dark waters lapping against the sides of the boat created a monotonous sound. Under different circumstances the motion of waves making the boat rock could easily put me to sleep. Yet watching the water now and River, I could only hope it wasn't his last nap. The dark, inky river continued flowing beneath the ground while the burned trees stood like unseeing soldiers, and the red sky burned gloomily above us.

I glanced back at the skeletal remains of the couple sitting in their burned chairs, facing each other, and I wondered what had happened to them. I hoped they were madly in love until their last moments together. They had died holding each other's hands, and it amazed me they had stayed in that same position for however many years, and nothing had disturbed them.

A wind blew through their bony ribs and skull, creating a hollow whistling sound. At least these two had died together, in each other's arms. I wondered who had killed them and why. The strange thing, or rather for this world it was strange, what were they doing sitting on this hill that overlooked the forest of dead trees and a black, thick stream that went everywhere.

'Look closer, Scout,' Jake said inside my head, pulling me out of my thoughts. *'Look.'*

"What? What must I look at?" I asked, sounding more annoyed than I wanted to be.

'Here.' Jake hovered above the one skeleton, and I glanced at the ribs. And there, in fine engraved detail, was hope.

Chapter Sixteen

A heart of glass will destroy these shackles made of bones.

Those were the words engraved on the ribs of the smaller of the two skeletons, which I assumed was female.

"What does that mean?" I asked, confused by the stupid riddle.

'Maybe you need to use the dragon's heart on them, and not as an entrance into the garden.'

"Jake, you smart little crow, you. Why didn't you say so before."

Jake made a strange gargle sound that if he was human, would be like a harrumph, followed by the rolling of his eyes.

I left Jake by the skeleton couple and ran down to the boat. River remained where I'd left him, but I couldn't tell if he was breathing. I rested my hand near his mouth and felt his warm shallow breath and sighed with relief. I moved his hair out of his face and watched him breathe for a moment before taking the backpack with the glass dragon heart.

Carefully climbing out, I stood beside the boat and watched him. He didn't stir and that deep hollow feeling returned. I blinked back tears and walked slowly up the hill. My thoughts crashed from us succeeding somehow to not and losing River forever. I stared at the couple on their chairs and for a moment imagined River and me growing old together. I choked on the sob and swallowed hard.

When I finally reached the skeletons, Jake sat on the chairback of the male skeleton. *'How is he doing?'*

"Not great," I said, kneeling in front of the two chairs. "Now, let's see how we can use this." I removed the glass dragon heart from the backpack with one hand and slowly brought it near the skeletons. When nothing happened, I stood up. Again, nothing happened when I waved it over their skulls, arms, near their legs and feet.

'Hold it near the female,' Jake said inside my head and hopped onto the other skeleton with the inscription on her ribs.

I stepped closer, bringing the glass heart near her ribs. The tip of the heart grazed the bone, sending vibrations up my shoulder and my arms pebbled. Jake flapped his wings, moving farther away.

"That felt weird," I said, stepping close enough that my foot touched the chair leg. I moved my hand under her rib cage, as if placing the dragon's heart in the spot where her heart was meant to be, and the magnetic force surrounding her bony ribs kicked up a notch, yanking the glass heart out of my hands.

I jerked back in fright as the glass heart hovered in her bony chest. Jake flew overhead, squawking. The glass heart started beating, the sound reverberating in my chest; the weird part was the glass heart started beating in time with mine. I stepped farther backward when the female skeleton sat upright, letting go of her partner's bony fingers, and her skull turned to me. If she had lips, I hoped she was smiling.

I opened my mouth to say something but swallowed my words when organs manifested inside her ribcage, followed by muscles, veins, tissue, fat, eyes, cartilage, and then skin. When she was a fully formed living human, she smiled, her eyes twinkling, then reached for the male skeleton. Just as her body had formed, so did his. Moments passed and then two normal looking humans sat before me, staring at me like nothing had happened. That only moments before they were just bones sitting in a chair.

"Thank you," the female said, dusting a leaf off her naked thigh. "We've been waiting for years for someone brave enough to find us."

I cleared my throat. "Excuse me. You've been here for years? What happened?"

She smiled, jerking her chin at her partner. "He didn't ask for directions—"

I burst out laughing. A tear slid down my cheek, and the muscles in my shoulders relaxed. These last couple of minutes had filled me with so much tension that I welcomed her humor.

"Liar," the male said. "Never trust what Mother Nature says about me." He harrumphed, folding his arms across his large, naked chest.

Mother Nature! I glanced at her and back at River, and my heart swelled with hope once more.

"See what you've done," Mother Nature said, "now she's alarmed."

"No, I'm just glad I found you. We've been looking all over for you. We need your help."

"Your friend in the boat?"

"Yes, can you help him?"

"I'm a little rusty," she said, giggling, "but I'm sure I can do something. But first, who are you?"

I bit my lip. I became wary, unsure whether I could tell her who my father was or where I was from. Just now, that alone had negative consequences for both myself and River.

"What is it, child?" she asked kindly, like a mother would ask a child. "Do not be afraid to tell me who you are. I have no quarrel with anyone—"

"Except one person," the man said.

"Shh, my love, let her tell her story."

I knew I had to just get it over and done with and tell her. Her sons were my half-brothers, therefore I doubted I would be in any danger. But... I sighed. "My name is Scout, my mother is Blaire and father is Victor, Lord of the Underworld."

Mother Nature smiled kindly. "I know Victor very well. Do you know where his brother Seth is?"

I shook my head. "No, everyone is looking for him, even Dad."

Something flickered in her green eyes. She glanced at her partner and held out her hands for him to take. He grabbed her hands like his life depended on it and they stood up as one. It was only then did I fully appreciate their naked bodies, but it didn't bother me. I was comfortable with my body and if someone wanted to walk around naked, who was I to judge or complain.

"For freeing us from the prison Seth put us in. Tell me,

what is wrong with your friend?" Mother Nature said, nestling her body under her partner's arm and wrapping her arms around his waist.

I explained how River and I helped my father and, in the process, they had sent River to Antarctica, but not without injury.

"He lost his memory, can't feel the ties to your father, has aged, and possibly dying," she said. I nodded. Mother Nature let go of her partner's hand, tucked brown hair behind her ear, and sashayed to the boat with confidence.

As we followed her to the boat, I said, "Who are you? If you don't mind me asking?"

"I'm Gerald," he said, smiling mischievously. "And apparently Seth wants me dead, the jealous, lying, cheating son of the devil." Anger radiated off him in waves. "And when I get my hands on him," he raised both hands and started choking the air in front of him, "he's going to pay for what he did to us. And for years, might I add. Stuck in this nothingness unable to go anywhere or ask for help."

"Quit complaining," Mother Nature said as she stepped inside the boat. "I've had to listen to you bicker for far too long. It's enough now."

Gerald sighed loudly and rolled his eyes, but he wasn't angry. The smile on his face told me he enjoyed upsetting Mother Nature. At least he had a sense of humor, too.

"Did Seth know you were here all along?" I asked, remembering that Seth had been searching for Mother Nature. If he did this to them, then he would know where they were.

"No, he didn't know where we were, but he did poison us," Gerald said. He was neither handsome nor ugly; he had nondescript features that were common, nothing about him stood out except the color of his eyes; yellow, bordering on golden. I'd only seen eyes similar to his, and those belonged to Christian, my mother's other boyfriend.

"You're staring," he said, and I glanced away. He burst out laughing, which made me laugh. "Don't worry, I know it's the eyes. No lady can resist them—"

Mother Nature gave him a look that quickly squashed the rest of his sentence. "Behave. Now stop pestering Scout and give me a hand."

"Yes, my lady." Gerald winked at me and went to his woman. He rubbed her back before climbing inside the boat with her. "What do you need me to do?"

"Lift him up and let him rest against your chest."

Gerald turned to me and said, "Will your man have a hissy fit if he wakes and a naked man is holding him?"

I smiled. "No, he has no issues in that department." River had told me he had kissed a man once when he was out of college, but he still preferred the intimate touch of a woman.

"Good, because the last thing I need now is a black eye or two." Gerald reached for River, picked him up and pulled him over his naked body and sat down. He shifted a bit until he was comfortable holding him. "Ready when you are, love."

Mother Nature clapped her hands together and rubbed, blowing into her hands for warmth. She did this a few times and each time she clapped, a blue flame appeared, and when she blew into her hands, a white light emitted from her open lips.

Her actions reminded me of my mother, whose white aura was one of her powers. She could heal people with it, absorb other people's powers, and then use it whenever she wanted. I wondered if Mother Nature had that same ability.

Mother Nature glanced at me when I thought this and winked, as if confirming my thoughts. Then she unzipped River's jacket, loosening the buttons of his shirt and opening it, revealing his pale, barely moving chest.

A sob caught in my throat, and I did everything I could to swallow it. Not wanting to cry now, I hugged myself and moved so that I could see River's face. I needed to be strong for him, and I wanted him to see a friendly face the moment he woke up.

Mother Nature sat beside River and Gerald, pressing her hands against his chest and blue flames came out of her hands and into him like she was a human defibrillator. She did this over and over. River's chest rose and fell each time, but he didn't wake. Then she closed her eyes and her hands hovered just above his chest.

I saw no movement from River; he wasn't even breathing. I wanted to go to him and hold him in my arms while he died, but something told me to wait. That I needed to give Mother Nature space to do what she needed.

I covered my mouth with my hand to stifle a cry and allowed the tears to fall.

Mother Nature said words I didn't understand. The wind had increased and blew in all directions. It felt as though we were in the middle of a tornado. Gerald held River tightly, and he too closed his eyes, his lips moving in time with Mother Nature's. And then they glowed in unison; a faint white, golden glow surrounding them. The glow moved through them, around them and then from Mother Nature's hands into River's chest.

I held my breath, waiting, watching. My anxiety spiked tenfold, and I wiped tears away so that I could see better.

Then a big, bright ball of flames blasted me backward and into the black, inky water.

Chapter Seventeen

I landed with my bum in the shallow part of the black water, sending black drops all over my clothing, hair, and face. My hands were stuck in the black mud and when I pulled them out, I pulled some of the black gunk with me. I shook my hands and most of it came off, but some were stuck underneath my nails. Then I felt heat beat against my face and chest. I forgot about the black water and sand and saw River levitating in the air like the big, flaming skeleton I knew and loved.

"River!" I said, crawling out of the mud and using the boat to help me stand on shaky legs. A nervousness swept through me as I watched in awe.

River hovered in the air like a ball of flames, reminding me of the sun. He arched his back with his legs and arms spread wide. He was in his human form and burned beautifully; the blue, yellow, and red flames pulsing out of his body warmed my skin.

Tears of happiness streamed down my face as I watched the man I loved come back to life.

Gerald and Mother Nature stood on one side, admiring the view.

Jake flew to me and perched on my shoulder. *'Ick,'* Jake said in my head. *'This stuff is gross… and it smells.'* Jake flew to a nearby branch.

'Chicken,' I thought back to him, and wiped the black mud off my face, then gave up when I was putting more of it back on than taking off.

River continued hovering like a ball of light, then slowly transformed into his skeleton, alive with those angry flames I knew so well. Slowly, he levitated back to the ground and his flames died down. He morphed back into his human form; but it was no longer the young River I knew, but the one who had aged so quickly. I didn't pity him; everything he did in his past was bound to catch up with him, like now. At least he was himself once more.

"Do you remember me?" I asked carefully, desperately wanting to know the answer but also afraid of what it would be. My heart thundered in my chest. My palms were sweating, and I wiped them on my pants, but forgot everything was still full of black mud.

"Hey, Peanut," River said, and my heart melted. He started calling me Peanut six months into our relationship and I loved how it made me feel. Which girlfriend didn't like the cute nickname her doting boyfriend gave her? Unfortunately, I no longer deserved that nickname because we weren't together, yet the sound of his voice calling me that filled me with hope.

I ran to him, crushing him with my hug, and then my lips found his. I clung to him, never wanting to leave his side again. River wrapped an arm around my waist while his other grabbed loose hair. He pulled gently, pulling my head back slightly, and my lips parted for him. He pressed his lips against mine again, his tongue exploring my mouth. The heat from his body enveloped mine, and I clawed at his jacket, pulling him closer to my body. It was a combination of sexual heat that was both gentle yet dominating.

Someone cleared their throat.

My thoughts returned to the now and we slowly let go of each other like a teenage couple caught by their parents.

"I can see you are yourself again," Mother Nature said, grinning.

River nodded. "Yes, Ma'am. Thank you for saving me."

"My dear," Mother Nature said. "Thank the brave girl beside you. Nobody loves you as much as she does. She's an over-thinker and one thing I know about them is they thought of every reason not to love you. So, if she says she loves you, believe her. And promise me one thing," she didn't wait for River to respond, and continued, "that you'll take care of this one." She reached for me, and her hands sparkled near my face. I shut my eyes tightly as wind, water, and air whipped around me. When I opened my eyes again, I was clean, even my clothing was dry.

"Thank you," I said, beaming from ear to ear. "Do you know of an easier way out of here?"

———————

There was no easy exit from this world, so we had to leave the same way we had entered. Therefore, we followed Mother Nature and Gerald through the strange burned-out garden, then through the weeping willows and circular trees. Nothing had changed from when we were first here; not that I was expecting anything to change, but I couldn't help the feeling of being watched as we followed the uneven path, missing all the booby traps. I brushed the willow trees out of my face and couldn't remember doing this when we had first walked here.

River squeezed my hand, and I looked at him, my smile stretching my face in two. "You doing okay?" I asked for the millionth time.

"Yes, all good," he said, grinning. Then his smile faded when mine did. "What's wrong?"

I didn't want to say, but he would find out. "You aged a little during your time here and well," I glanced away so he couldn't see the tears in my eyes, "you look your forty-five years and I'm…" I left my words trailing. We had an age gap of twenty years, and I didn't know if it was something he wanted, or even myself. Then I started wondering what others would say when they found out.

"Twenty years younger?" he said gently, finishing my sentence. Then he stopped walking, pulling me to one side, and rested his hands on my shoulders. "I love you, Scout," he said, his eyes penetrating mine. "The years between us mean nothing, and you shouldn't care what others think. I'm in my late forties and you are in your twenties, so what? Why should that bother us? I love you and you love me." I nodded, my smile reaching my eyes again. "And we had a bump in the road once before and we sorted it out so we can manage anything that comes our way. I love you and that's all that matters."

He pulled me into an embrace and kissed the top of my head. There was something wonderful about the man I loved kissing the top of my head or my forehead. To me, it was a symbol of his love, devotion, and care, all bundled up in that one delegate kiss.

I hugged him tightly then when he let go; I did too, but not before kissing his chest. Then I rocked onto my toes, wrapped my arms around his neck, and kissed him. I bruised his lips with mine and I wanted nothing more than to make love to him here and now.

Then someone cleared their throat. "As much as I love watching this sexual tension unfold, we have to get going," Gerald said with a smirk. "The wind has changed, and I don't know about you, but Mother Nature and I need clothes, food, and a safe place to rest."

"Can't Mother Nature conjure clothing like she did when she cleaned the mud off of me and dried my clothing?" I let go of River's neck and reached for his hand. I wasn't quite ready to let go of him completely, just now he disappeared, and all this was a bad dream.

"She could, but it depleted her energy helping him," Gerald said, glancing in River's direction. "Let's go, the Town Square is only a stone's throw away."

Chapter Eighteen

Once we reached the Town Square, Gerald found clothing for himself and Mother Nature. The locals didn't notice us again, even when we stole clothing and food. I couldn't help but wonder whether they were real and what their purpose was if they weren't. They seemed oblivious to the fact that we walked among them, spoke loud enough for them to hear us clearly, yet they did nothing.

Instead of climbing up the ladder we had used to enter the Town Square, Mother Nature found an alternative path through the maze to get to the House of Relativity. Once inside, we traversed up flights of stairs, turned corners and up another set of stairs. When I glanced around, I realized we were upside down and almost jumped onto River's back for fear of falling over. Luckily, he realized my dilemma and told me to close my eyes and to hold onto his arm.

A second time today I caught myself staring at him, but it was because I was so grateful he was okay. When I slipped my hand into his, my body reacted to his touch. It was a binding of my core to his, my heart to his, our souls to each other. It was a place that felt safe, and comforting, and… it felt like home; where all my attempts to escape reality ceased.

I walked blindly beside him up and down stairs. Doors opened and closed. And when River told me to finally open my eyes, we were at the main entrance/exit of the Maze. We were just about to cross the threshold into the Mammoth Cave when groaning sounded behind us, followed by loud screaming.

We spun around, coming face to face with a large, hairy, ape-looking man and a pale woman with white hair who wore a light blue dress. The woman stared with black eyes at the men and screamed. Her high pitch screams pierced my eardrums, and I was sure they were about to explode. The men flew against the hedges while Mother Nature and I stood holding our ears closed.

The large hairy ape-man groaned and closed the distance. Pus and chunks of flesh fell from its shoulder and a putrid stench assaulted my olfactory senses. I struggled to keep my ears and nose closed from the screams and stink.

Mother Nature scowled at the pale woman screaming at us, stood straight, and approached her in a flash of light. She slammed her fist into the woman's neck, silencing her. When she doubled over, Mother Nature elbowed her back, breaking it. She crumpled to the ground like a rag doll, moaning. At least she was no longer screaming.

Just as the hairy ape-man was about to wrap his large decomposing claws around Mother Nature's neck, I pushed him out of the way and his soul flew out. My large black wings opened behind me and before his soul could return, I ripped his pus-festering head from his body. His soul cried out silently and I called the Ferryman to collect him.

The pale woman used her arms to crawl back to

Mother Nature, trying desperately to claw at her ankles. I flew into her before she could scream one last time. Her soul flew out of her body just as quickly and it hit the Ferryman's boat. But before she could return to her broken body, he scooped her soul up too, locking both souls in place. He thanked us, and he went on his way again.

Mother Nature tipped her head in thanks, and said, "What the hell was that?"

"I think a banshee and a zombi-yeti?" I said, looking at the surrounding carnage.

"Good grief," Mother Nature said, "I've never encountered anything like that before."

"Me neither."

Movement sounded behind us.

"Thanks for the help, gents, but we got this covered," I said jokingly when River approached, rubbing the back of his head.

"Jeez, that was some screech," River said, dusting sand off his shoulders. He and Gerald had flown into a wall and had crumpled into the sand below. "What tells you she didn't like men?"

I giggled, agreeing with him.

Gerald closed the gap with Mother Nature, wrapping his meaty arms around her waist and bringing her closer. He dipped her to one side like they were dancing and kissed up her neck. When he found her mouth, she moaned with pleasure.

"They need a room," River said, "and fast."

———

We stopped by the small rocky waterfall and pond where the woman with dark hair had told us what to do. We washed our faces, quenched our thirst, and enjoyed a quiet moment's rest.

Gerald jumped up to attack when we heard footsteps, but it was only the Lady of the Garden. She sauntered toward Mother Nature, not tearing her eyes away from her.

"Moon," Mother Nature said, standing. "How kind of you to see us out. If only you were this gracious when we had first arrived."

"Sister, darling, don't take everything personally. You know I had to say something, or he'd destroy everything we had worked so hard to create." She raised her arms.

"You betrayed your own sister." Mother Nature shook her head in disgust. "How could you?"

Moon visibly relaxed and glanced down. Then she glanced up at River and me. "They rescued you."

"Years later." Mother Nature closed the gap, standing so close to Moon that their breasts touched. Gerald stood behind Mother Nature in a protective stance. "You knew how to release me from his curse, yet you did nothing."

"I didn't know what he would do. I was afraid he was watching me or had a demon monitoring me. Seth is an awful demon and yes, I shouldn't have said anything to him, but he threatened everyone in these underground worlds. I knew you would survive, and you did. But everyone else would've perished." Moon reached for Mother Nature, who didn't push her away. Knowing Mother Nature wouldn't reject her, Moon pulled her sister into a loving hug.

Moments passed and their touching embrace ended with them both in tears; golden tears that shone brightly then evaporated into the air, forming a bright outline of their bodies. They looked like they had sprinkled pixy dust all over themselves and were about to fly away, but they didn't. They let go of each other but continued staring into the other's eyes as if silently communicating.

"Right," Moon said, neatening her dress. "Get out now. That monster is still looking for you."

Mother Nature didn't have to be told twice. She grabbed Gerald's hand and fast-walked to the exit with us close behind. We passed the sweet-smelling flower garden, then the vegetable garden, and stopped at the secret door.

I turned back and marveled at the Mammoth Cave. Our journey into the earth and discovering these underground worlds was an experience I wished my mother could enjoy, but for once I was the one who could share something she knew nothing about.

River pulled my arm to let me know he was about to walk through the secret door. I glanced up at him and smiled, my heart pounding in my chest. And everything we had gone through had been worth it; me seeing his sweet smile and those dark brown eyes that held his memory was worth it. He was back again, and I hoped we could spend the rest of our days together.

Chapter Nineteen

We had found an alternative route to the surface, otherwise climbing up that slide would've been disastrous. River closed the lid to the secret door near the pond with a loud thud, while Mother Nature and Gerald waited patiently for us.

In the distance, people were screaming, yelling, and holding items in their hands. River and I glanced at each other with *'what happened'* expressions and then at Mother Nature.

"We have to go," Mother Nature said. "We will find you and help you get out, but right now, they can't know who we are. I hope you understand." Her parting words were only a slight comfort. They bolted for a copse of trees to our far left, and although I didn't know why the townsfolk were upset with us, I hoped they didn't see Mother Nature or Gerald fleeing.

The townsfolk approached with crazed determination, holding pitchforks and torches. What I couldn't understand was why we were about to be tarred and feathered by them.

"Scout," Henry said in a loud, serious tone that made my forearms pebble. He closed the gap and stood in front of me wearing a scary expression. "You are being charged with the murder of Neville, Miss Harriet, and Mikey."

"What? How? I haven't even been here," I pleaded, pushing Henry's hands away from me.

"Irrelevant, you are new to our town and ever since you arrived, people have been dying. It's one reason we don't have crows here. They bring death and destruction. And you," he was quiet for a moment, then added, "have brought nothing but death to our town."

"But it wasn't me, Henry. You know this. I've been helping River gain his memory back."

Henry puffed out his chest. He probably anointed himself sheriff for the day. He glanced at River, doing a double take when he realized River had aged significantly, but he said nothing about it. Then he turned those dark eyes on me and said, "Everyone has asked that I take you in for questioning. It's that or we offer you to the well."

"The well? The well Neville fed daily?" I asked. Henry nodded. "What's down that well? No, never mind. I don't want to know." I pushed Henry's hand away when he tried to cuff my wrists together. "Don't, it's unnecessary. I will go willingly." Then I turned to River. "You need to find my mother or father." I shrugged out of my backpack that had my phone and handed it to River. I knew my father wouldn't be around to help. He had his own issues to take care of, and I wasn't sure whether Mother Nature would return and free me. If not, hopefully my mom could assist.

Henry brought me back to the hotel and locked me inside a room aptly named *Terror Gate*. I tried not to show how scared I was, but from the smirk on Henry's face, I'd failed. The room was small, and in a morbid gray color. It was big enough for one person; it had a desk and a chair with little space around it. There were no windows or air vents, only one light fixture in the middle of the ceiling that flickered.

I didn't know what these demons would do to me now that they thought I killed their people. It wasn't me, but I didn't know how to show them without proof.

River couldn't stay with me. Before Henry brought me to this room, I watched River get into the elevator and the doors closed. It felt like a life sentence had just sealed my fate as I stood there all alone, shivering, as he left me. I shouldn't take him leaving personally, but I did. It wasn't River's fault they didn't allow him to keep me company. Thank goodness River's memory had returned, so when he got back to his suite, he knew what he needed to do.

After a few minutes, the adrenaline had worn off and my hands started shaking. I pulled out the chair and almost sat down. I crouched to get a closer look, then pushed the chair away. They had glued tiny spikes onto the chair so that whoever sat down would get stabbed by multiple tiny swords, causing the person to bleed profusely.

Needing to sit, I first inspected the table, then wiped it with my hands. There were no spikes, poisonous powder, or anything visible I could find. I checked the legs and moved the table away from the chair. I first tested whether it could handle my weight, then I climbed onto the table and laid down with my hands above my head.

Even with my eyes closed, the flickering light bothered me. I tried covering my eyes with one hand, and it still irritated me. I sighed wearily. There was no point in getting angry or sad. Whatever happened next, I just needed to believe that River or Mother Nature would help me.

"Don't trust him," said someone nearby. I glanced around, but it was only me inside this tiny cell. "Don't trust him," she said again, and I bolted upright. I turned the other way, coming face to face with the woman in the bathtub. Her dreamlike features floating in and out of reality. "Don't believe his lies."

I jerked awake when the door swung open and slammed against the wall. Henry entered like storm clouds about to rain all over me. I sat up, scooting to the far side of the small table, farther away from him.

Henry raised his hand and dropped a file on the table beside my legs. "It's not pretty, Scout," he said, stepping backward and folding his arms across his chest. He had folded his shirt above his elbow and his thick tattoos spelling "MAKE ME" glowered at me, too.

I picked up the folder and opened it. River usually protected me when he needed to do something awful, but since working with Mom and Ralph, I'd seen some pretty gruesome things. The pictures I saw in that folder made my brain shut down. Although Neville had just collapsed and died, what happened to him later was terrible; his body had burst open with parasites crawling on, in, and between his organs. The mortician had to use a flamethrower to kill those wiggly things.

I shuddered, turning the pages quickly. Mikey, the lumberjack with bright red hair and beard, had bled from every orifice. When the mortician opened his chest cavity, he found parasites different from the ones inside of Neville. His body had to be cremated, too.

Lastly Miss Harriet, the gray-haired old lady with the bun in her hair, had died by one of her own bread rolls.

Apparently, this bread roll was so old and so hard, they discovered her with it lodged in her throat. I shook my head. How could anyone use it as a weapon? After browsing the photos, I noted there were scratch marks on the inside of her right wrist, and they found pieces of skin underneath her left fingernails. Again, the mortician discovered small parasites when he opened her cranium.

"Parasites, Henry, it's parasites. How on earth can I get all these different parasites inside them? I'm not a scientist. I work with my mother as a legal monster assassin. And although I was only here for a short time, I considered Neville my friend. He helped me survive the White Devil when I first arrived. Why would I kill him or the other two? It made little sense." I rambled on and on, and Henry just watched me like a hawk.

Henry coughed into his meaty fist and pushed away from the wall. He corrected the photos and reports and picked up the folder. "I believe you, Scout, but these people want blood. Your blood. Unless..."

"Unless what?" I asked, curious what that 'unless' meant.

Henry opened his mouth when the chanting started, cutting his sentence.

"Praise white devil for protecting us..." said the crowd nearby. A glaze of sweat covered my body, knowing they were outside that door, and they were thirsty for my blood. It was their lunch time feeding ritual, and I was their meal. "...and shielding us from the outside world. With this hand, we raise your praises. Our cups will never empty, for you always provide..." I swallowed hard, climbing off the table, and standing behind it. If they rushed the room, I would use it as a weapon. "...and with our lips, we'll drink from your vein..." I flinched when someone banged against the door. "…Our souls forever yours."

Silence.

I stood straight, and my black wings expanded. Henry arched both eyebrows, clearly surprised by my display. He tucked the folder behind his back and into his pants, keeping it secure.

Mumbling disrupted the ear shattering silence. The doorknob turned, but the door didn't open.

My heart thumped loudly in my chest. Sweat peppered my forehead.

Click clacking sounded against the floors, and I glanced nervously at Henry, who shrugged.

Someone spoke in hushed tones, followed by shuffling. The doorknob turned. I levitated. My wings keeping me airborne. The door opened. I held my breath. And a woman with long dark hair sauntered inside.

Chapter Twenty

The woman entered, turning her head at an angle so that only I could see her wink. Mother Nature? I hoped so. Unless my mom knew someone who could get here quicker than she could, and they were here to help get me out.

"I'm Tiffany," she said, approaching the table. "Are you the sheriff of this godforsaken ice-town?" she asked angrily, standing with her back close to me. She had one hand behind her back, which she slowly opened. In her palm was a key.

Not wanting to arouse suspicion, I grabbed the key carefully and pocketed it, then stood beside her.

"Yes, ma'am," Henry said with a twang to his accent. He grinned stupidly at her. When his eyes flittered to me, his grin fell off his face. He cleared his throat and folded his arms again. "We have three dead people, and she was the only one new in our town. Therefore—"

"Where's your proof that she did anything?"

"We—"

"Have nothing. You guys just want someone to blame

and she's it. How do you know that the creature you feed in that well isn't to blame for the parasites?"

I turned to ask her how she knew about the parasites or the creature in the well but swallowed my tongue when I saw the mesh behind her ear. She was wearing a wig.

"But she's—"

"Your scapegoat." *Tiffany* kept interrupting Henry, and I did everything I could not to cheer her on. She continued snapping back every time Henry opened his mouth, only muttering a word here or there.

After a few minutes of bantering, *Tiffany* was winning 20-0. Henry stood with a mouth full of teeth, nodding profusely.

"Okay, fine," Henry yelled, "just stop talking." He combed his fingers through his disheveled hair. "Let's go down to the well and you can see for yourself. The creature that lives there did not do this."

"Neither did my client," *Tiffany* said, pulling on her salmon-colored woolen cap. "Now where is my client's jacket. It's freezing out there." She turned to me and winked again.

Henry opened the door, and over his shoulder said, "Stay put." And slammed the door closed.

"Mom?"

"Close enough," she said, reaching for my hand and slowly opening the door. "Let's get out of here before he realizes you're gone."

The foyer was empty, but instead of running for the front door, we ran toward the far end near the office. *Tiffany* pushed open a swinging door, we entered the vacant kitchen, and headed for the exit.

"Use the key I gave you," she said. "I wasn't sure

whether he would give us a gap to escape, but this worked out even better than I expected."

I pulled out the key and unlocked the door. Slowly, she opened the door and stepped out into the snow. I flinched when a hand holding a jacket came into my view. Then I smiled when River showed his face, holding my backpack.

"Are you ready to get out of here?" he asked.

"Absolutely," I said, grabbing the jacket and slipping inside the warm clothing. I zipped up and sighed with relief. I was about to close my backpack when Jake popped his head out and squawked at me. "Hey buddy," I said, rubbing his head.

"Come," *Tiffany* said, dashing off into the distance.

"Was that…" I said.

"Yep, that was Mother Nature," River said, grinning. "She needed a disguise, and I think she did a pretty good job."

We closed the gap with *Tiffany*/Mother Nature, who raised her leg as if getting onto something, but there was nothing other than snow with more snow falling on top of us. I was about to tell her there was nothing there when a Jeep Wrangler materialized, and Gerald sat in the driver's seat.

"Your chauffeur has arrived," Gerald sang.

I ducked when gun shots rang and echoed around us. River swore beside me, throwing his duffle bag into the back of the Jeep. Mother Nature jumped inside and before I could climb into the backseat, River picked me up and threw me into the open back of the Jeep. I landed with a yelp and River jumped in beside me. His hands were glowing a fierce flame, and he yelled, "Go."

Gerald smashed the gas and took off. My head jerked forward, pain shooting down my spine, and I winced. The townsfolk exited the hotel like a swarm of angry bees. I watched in slow motion how they climbed out of their skins, kicking it off, and started running. Their run was unnaturally fast yet smooth, like they had Usain Bolt's speed, but their gait was slightly lopsided, like an ape.

"Faster!" I yelled, gripping the bar near my head so tightly my hands ached. Snow continued falling around us, and I had to keep wiping my eyes. The Jeep skidded to one side, then Gerald corrected our path, and we went faster.

Their pale, blotchy-red, scaly skins made them look otherworldly as they sprinted toward us. Their smooth heads melted the snow and their dark orbs for eyes were all trained on us. They were blood-thirsty, and we were their meal.

I called out to Father for help, but silence greeted me. Jake moved uneasily in my backpack. River turned his flaming skeleton their way, but he didn't go after them. There were too many of them for him to take on by himself, and I doubted it was in Mother Nature's nature to attack and hurt anyone. I knew little about Gerald and what he would or could do.

"Scout!" River yelled, bringing me out of my thoughts and just in time to see a creature climbing onto the Jeep on my side.

"No," I said through gritted teeth and kicked it in the face. The creature screeched, reminding me of the banshee we had encountered in the maze. Unfortunately, the kick to its face did nothing, and it snapped sharp teeth at me. I was holding on for safety reasons, but I also wanted to get rid of this creature before it took a bite out of me.

River battled his own creature, who was hanging onto the back of the Jeep near him.

My   smooth-skinned-teeth-chomping-fiend   pulled

himself up onto the side of the Jeep. Gripping the bar with one hand, I slammed my free palm into it, cracking a knuckle. I didn't know if these creatures had souls and when I touched it; nothing flew out of its body. I slammed my palm into it again and nothing. This creature was an empty shell.

The creature screamed once more and lunged at me. I pulled the knife from my backpack and slashed at the creature's wrist, severing it. The creature didn't register what I had done and when I kicked its chest; it thought it was still holding on, but it wasn't, and it went flying off the back and into the snow. I pried the creature's dead fingers from the Jeep and threw the hand overboard. And as a parting gift, the hand raised its middle finger, flipping me off before falling into the snow.

River battled his creature and got him off; it crashed into a house, knocking out one side.

"They don't have souls," I said.

"What?" River yelled.

"They don't have souls," I said, closer to his face. "They are soulless beings."

"They are being controlled by someone," Mother Nature said calmly in the front seat.

I glanced over my shoulder and blinked at her. "What do you mean by controlled? By whom?"

She shrugged. "But I have a good idea." Then she pointed right, and Gerald turned in that direction. We drove over a large bump, and I almost smacked my head against the bar. I turned to see where we were heading, and my jaw slackened. There was only a large, iced wall in front of us. There was nothing else here or nowhere to go. I couldn't understand where we were going, but if we continued on this route, we would hit the ice wall.

The creatures had given up. They stopped chasing us near that bump we had flown over and stared at us with murderous intent. Someone pushed his way through the creature-crowd and to the front. His dark gaze felt like shards of glass on my naked skin. The hairs on the back of my neck stood up as my skin ran cold.

"Henry's a little creepy," River said. "I wonder why they aren't chasing us."

"This is sacred ground," Mother Nature said, pointing to the right. "You've forgotten your way, my love," she said teasingly.

Gerald reached for Mother Nature's hand, holding it near his mouth, and kissed the top of it. "My love, you know I need you."

Chapter Twenty-One

"Where are we going?" I asked.

The Jeep came to a stop near the tallest iceberg I'd ever seen. The only difference was we weren't near any water.

In silence, Mother Nature and Gerald shared a knowing look and climbed out. "Follow us," she said, pulling off her dark wig. Her facial features morphed back into her normal face, and I did all I could not to stare openmouthed at her. She was a master of disguises. But I guess she had certain powers I knew nothing about.

Jake moved uncomfortably in my backpack, so I took him out, settling him on my shoulders.

'Where are we going?' he said in my head.

'No idea, buddy. No idea.'

Mother Nature and Gerald walked toward the iced wall with purpose. We followed slowly behind them. I glanced up at the gigantic wall of ice. Something sparkled, then moved. After a moment, a person standing on an ice balcony appeared, then he moved, disappearing into the ice again. I swallowed hard.

Up ahead, it looked like Mother Nature and Gerald were about to slam their faces into the ice wall, instead they walked through it and the wall became an iced tunnel.

"Wow," I said, blinking to make sure I saw correctly. As we entered the ice tunnel, a chilly breeze slammed into me, taking my breath away. I stood still for a second to catch my breath, my face burning from the cold.

"Here," Mother Nature said, handing me a scarf that she magically conjured up. "We're almost there." Her smile reached her emerald-colored eyes.

"What's going on?" I asked.

River reached for my hand, pulling me back to walk beside him. He shook his head and whispered, "They'll tell us when they're ready. For now, let's first see where we're going."

I pursed my lips, not liking this. They could take us somewhere dangerous, but if that were the case, they could've left us with Henry and his monsters. Dammit, I hated it when River was right. I sighed. At least we were safe from Henry and his soulless creatures, and wherever Mother Nature was taking us would be better than staying outside with them.

We traversed the cold, icy tunnel in silence except for the crunching of our boots against the ice. The tunnel was brightly lit, but there were no visible light fixtures anywhere, and it seemed to get colder the deeper we walked.

Mother Nature stopped outside a door and waited for us to catch up. "As you've realized Earth isn't exactly a big blue ball in the universe but flat and it has worlds within worlds below, worlds above, and worlds around," she pointed at the door we were about to enter, "and this giant wall of ice is the border enclosing the continents you're used to. Beyond the wall on the other side are the galaxies they taught you at school. Continents filled with other beings who may look different to you and I." She smiled kindly and her eyes sparkled. "Now you understand why they don't allow planes to fly anywhere near the Arctic (North Pole) or the Antarctic (South Pole)."

I blinked at Mother Nature as my mind processed her words and it all made sense. I'd seen articles and videos about planes being restricted from flying over certain areas. One video suggested there was a hole inside the South Pole that went straight through the Earth and connected to the North Pole, but if the Earth were flat, that hole could just be an entrance to another world. And perhaps it was those worlds River and I had just been to.

Naturally, conspiracy theorists all had their theories, and one never knew what to believe, but now that we had been there, I believed that there was more to our earth than they had taught us at school. I now knew there were other worlds closer than the stars and we already lived with other types of beings. It was all about perspective and being open to believing in different worlds or one could stay within the safety of their ignorant cocoons; we all had a choice.

"Shall we?" Gerald said, breaking my daydream. He held the door open, and Mother Nature entered first.

I entered the room next and could go no farther. It looked like ground control for the military; which military I did not know. River pushed me farther inside the room, grabbing my hand and leading me to one side where Mother Nature waited.

"River, go with Gerald while Scout and I will freshen up here," she said, pointing at another door with a picture of a female on it.

River kissed my temple, squeezed my hand, and

followed Gerald inside the Men's bathroom. "I'll see you now," he said with a wink.

I smiled, but it fell soon after he entered the bathroom, leaving me alone. I glanced over my shoulder at the monitors, large screens, and the people manning their stations. The only reason I said 'people' was I didn't know what they were because they wore white uniforms with a black screen over the place where their faces were meant to be. It was something out of a Sci-Fi movie and I rarely watched them.

"Scout?" Mother Nature said gently.

I turned around and followed her inside.

"You're probably overwhelmed by everything."

"You could say that," I said numbly, removing my backpack and placing it on a bench near lockers against one wall. Jake perched on top of the bag, his eyes watching mine.

"I know there's lots to process, but the war between supernaturals has been ongoing for so long I can't tell you how or where or why it began. It's just always been us against them. What I know is the good guys are winning. We're finally taking back what belongs to us and the humans."

"And the soulless creatures outside?"

"Are bad, obviously." She was quiet for a moment as she removed her top. "And Seth is controlling them."

"So even between them in the Underworld, they are fighting. It explains why my father hates him."

"Exactly. You must understand, I loved Seth once. But that was many, many, many years ago. And when I left, he simply couldn't let me go and I've been hiding ever since. Have you met your half-brothers yet?" she asked, changing the subject. I nodded; I was proud to call those pesky but funny and wonderful demons my brothers. "Then you know that I'm their mother."

I looked up at her, my top button half undone. "Yeah," I said, smiling. "I recently found out when we were helping my father."

She nodded in understanding. "Seth didn't know." She filled her tone with sadness that squeezed my heart. "He wanted more children, but I only gave him one son. I broke it off when his mean streak got worse, and he constantly threatened my life. Your father and I had a secret affair and secret sons and we told no one. When Seth was hunting me down and vowed to kill anyone in his way, Victor took the boys and hid them in his demon army. It was only recently that they found out about me."

"How do you know all this if you were stuck in that Nothingland Garden back there?"

"I still have connections to them, no matter where I go. They're my children." Her eyes held a hint of sadness. "I'm their mother, and we'll always have a bond. It was the only way for me to ensure their safety." Her smile reached her glistening eyes. "Now come, let's enjoy a nice hot shower and wash all the bad and ugliness of what we've just gone through away."

The water struck my bruised body like someone was massaging my aching muscles just a little too hard. It felt like I'd rolled down a steep hill with the number of bruises and sore muscles I had. After I washed my hair and used the conditioner that smelled of jasmine, I stood under the hot jets and allowed them to do their work.

Mother Nature was quick, and I didn't hear her leave. When I finally exited the shower, a pile of fresh clothing sat beside my backpack with Jake eating a bowl of fresh insects, a raw egg, vegetables, and some nuts.

"Hmm, that looks delicious," I said, fixing a towel on my head, and my stomach grumbled. "Seems I need to eat something, too."

"There's food waiting for you outside," someone said behind me, making me flinch. I spun around, clutching my towel to my chest. Standing by the door like a scary security guard stood a woman with two tight buns on the sides of her head; or rather double space buns. I stifled a giggle because she reminded me of the lead actress from the movie Space Balls.

"Oh, hi," I said, embarrassed. "I'm—"

"Scout," she said. "I know who you are," she added with contempt. "Just hurry up. Everybody is already eating." Just as stealthily as her entrance, she exited, closing the door behind her.

"That was creepy," I mumbled and started dressing.

'She brought me my meal, and it's delicious,' Jake said inside my head.

"Eat up, buddy. You worked hard for it."

Jake squawked and finished his food by the time I had dressed and was ready to eat. We left the bathroom and found a small dining hall next to the Men's bathroom. Everyone was feasting loudly.

When River lifted his head and saw me, he smiled; the smile that lifted my spirits. The smile that warmed me from my head to my toes. His soft lips had planted kisses all over my body. While his hands caressed my skin and my soul. I shouldn't put him on a pedestal, but he deserved to be there. He wasn't perfect, and now, even less so now that he had aged, but that didn't mean I didn't love him. It was the opposite; he was perfectly imperfect for me, and I loved him.

In this moment, I realized I didn't want to be without

him, and would gladly be with him for the rest of my life. I'd do whatever it took to keep him in my life, whether as a lover or as best friends. He would continue working for my father until his contract was completed, and until then we would make something work; whatever that something was, I didn't know.

My stomach grumbled. But right now, I needed food.

I placed my backpack on the chair near River, picked up a plate and filled it with food that was spread out on trays. This was normal human food, not that stuff my father's creepy-monster-chef usually prepared in the Underworld. I could eat this food all day long. I sat beside River and forked some food into my mouth, but I stopped chewing when Mother Nature said that Henry and the creatures were about to attack.

Chapter Twenty-Two

I devoured a hotdog, three thin slices of meat, a spoonful of mash and gravy, then downed my cold coffee. River waited for me with my backpack by the door, handing it to me when I reached him.

"You ready?" he asked.

"No, but let's do this." I didn't know what was about to happen, but I'd give it my best.

We entered the room where all the monitors blinked violently at us.

Mother Nature stood with Gerald near the armory. The weapons they were handing out were not of the normal variety I was used to. These looked like Sci-Fi space guns. They were black with strange gadgets on top.

"It will neutralize them," Mother Nature said, handing us a weapon each, "and shock us, so be careful where you point them."

I slung the weapon over my shoulder and followed Gerald out a different door to that which we had used to enter. We stood at the back and in front of us were soldiers in black gear from head to toe. They each wore a helmet with the visor showing their vitals on one side, along with heat sensing visuals for anyone approaching.

The men in front of us said something to each other and they roared with laughter, which made me smile. At least they were a cheerful bunch of killer soldiers about to go into battle.

The soldiers cocked their weapons and stood at attention. Their movements were sharp and quick, and they stood as one, making me want to stand at attention, too. Their movements forced us to back up, giving them space while their Commander gave further instructions.

I stood in front of River and held onto his pants. He squeezed my shoulders and kissed the top of my head. "Everything will be all right," he said near the shell of my ear, sending goosebumps down my shoulders and back. "I'm sure my angry flames will wipe them out."

I raised my chin, resting my head against his chest, and smiled. "Goodie, then we can go for ice-cream afterward."

"Haha, definitely." He kissed me again.

I stood straight as Mother Nature passed us with determination stamped all over her face. She had already mentioned that Seth may be the one controlling Henry and the soulless creatures and from her expression, she would love to stop him once and for all. She stopped by the exit with the Commander and whispered into his ear. He nodded, glanced our way, and nodded again. He opened the door and instructed the first person to exit. Then, one by one, each soldier disappeared into a freezing blizzard.

I shivered at the door. Mother Nature's arm was up, blocking our way. "When you use the weapon on those creatures," she said, "aim for their heads." Then she looked at River, "your flames will come in handy, but try not to hurt any of our people." She patted his shoulder.

"Yes, Ma'am," River said and exploded into his angry flames. The fire within him raged around him, but it burned nothing and no one nearby. Unless he wanted it to burn someone.

River exited next and held out his hand. I reached for him, gripping his hand, and stepped outside. The snow whipped me from all sides, forcing me to close my eyes even though I wore ski goggles.

Shots fired overhead. Cold white flakes blew around us. I pursed my lips, tasting salt. River squeezed my hand as we traversed on the outskirts of the fight. Monsters clawed at the soldiers who fired back, blowing arms and heads off their bodies, but they didn't stop advancing. The creatures kept fighting, kept pushing their way forward even if it was only a leg rolling in the snow to get to the entrance.

River raised his fiery fist and slowly bringing it down, setting that rolling leg and the lower half of a creature on fire. I counted to ten, and the limbs burned to ash, then dissolved into the snow.

I glanced to the right and flinched. An arm that was severed at the shoulder used its fingers to crawl across the thick snow, leaving a bloody trail. River stood on the knuckles and his flames licked the wrist, setting it on fire.

A creature screamed when a soldier sliced it in half. Heat beat on my left-hand side and there stood Gerald with his own flamethrower. He kicked a creature in the chest and when it crashed to the ground; he burned it before it could retaliate. Within seconds it became crispy, then ash and melted into the snow.

I held my knife in my left hand in case anyone tried attacking us while I held River's left hand with my right. He burned limbs and creatures continuously and through all that he gripped my hand, not letting go of me.

A creature got through two soldiers and advanced toward Mother Nature, who stood near the door with her weapon in hand. I suspected she was the last to protect the entrance. The creature passed me, and I swiped at it, cutting it from its cheek, neck, and down its back. It stopped and turned its dark eyes on me. It salivated, spittle dripping down its chin. The sun glowed dimly through the snowstorm, outlining its body in a sparkly shine. My body stiffened. River stopped moving; his flames beat on my right-hand side. The creature lunged at me. I stuck out my left arm; the knife slicing into its abdomen. It didn't stop there. It continued reaching for me and my hand sunk deeper into its soft, squishy abdomen until my hand became lodged inside. River spun around me, blocking the creature's fists, and struck it with his elbow. The creature stumbled backward, my hand and knife slipping out of it, and before he could attack, River blasted him with fire.

"Thank you," I said, shaking out my left arm and dark maroon liquid sprayed everywhere. I rocked onto my tiptoes and kissed him quickly before another creature came at us.

I glanced around and so far our team was winning. There were heaps of bodies covering the snow in dark maroon while Gerald burned one after the other, ensuring none of them could come back to life.

A siren sounded above us. Right at the top of the ice wall was a lookout, sounding danger. Mother Nature yelled something I couldn't understand. Gerald continued burning bodies. The soldiers moved through the creatures like bull-dozers. It relieved me they were so easy to defeat. But I couldn't understand why we were on high alert.

"Run, Scout!" River yelled beside me, pulling my arm.

Mother Nature called us over. Her screams were loud, but I heard no words.

The sirens continued sounding above us.

The snow pelted our bodies as we sprinted across the snow.

I glanced over my shoulder and stopped. River yanked on my arm, but I couldn't move. The White Devil Neville was so scared of was fast approaching. I couldn't understand what had scared him other than the sound it made, but I understood now. I watched the White Devil approach in spectacular awe. It was the Devil's snowstorm. Hell's wind. Lucifer's elements. An evil thing that was nothing yet everything. It picked up the remaining soldiers and obliterated their bodies with its internal hurricane, leaving the area covered in red.

"Scout!" River yelled beside me, but I stood mesmerized by the show. He pulled on my arm, and I fell over, but he caught me before I crashed to the ground. He threw me over his shoulder and ran with me.

Gerald caught up, passing us as he entered the safety of the ice wall. The rest of the soldiers retreated as the White Devil lifted those remaining, grating their bodies against its wind, scattering their bloody remains everywhere.

But that's not what frightened me. It was the creature running with the White Devil.

Chapter Twenty-Three

Mother Nature slammed the door shut as the angry White Devil slammed against the door, scrapping its sharp elements against the heavy metal, followed by its deep growling wind.

I stood by the door, staring at it numbly. My arms hung limply at my sides like someone had cut them off at the sockets. Unable to move, all I could do was listen to the ominous cries of the White Devil, and its wind beating against the ice wall, creating a cacophony of angry cries.

"Scout? Peanut, are you okay?" River asked beside me. He sounded dreamlike as he turned me to look him in the eyes. "Focus on me," he said. I stared at his chest but heard nothing else. When he reached for my chin and raised my head, my eyes found his and I could focus. "Are you okay?" he asked again.

I could only nod.

"Are you hurt?"

I shook my head and shrugged. I didn't know. Nothing hurt, but that didn't mean I had no damage. I felt numb.

"She's in shock," Mother Nature said, approaching. "Let me help." She raised her hands and closed the gap. She pressed her left hand against my forehead, her right against my abdomen. The warmth from both of her hands pierced my body like an electric shock, almost sending me backward, but River was there to keep me upright. "Can you pick her up?"

"Yeah."

The next moment, my eyes closed, and River picked me up.

"Bring her here," Mother Nature said. "That's it. You can put her here."

I felt something soft against my back, then my feet, and then a pillow underneath my head. The weight of darkness kept my eyes closed and my mind quiet. I thought of nothing but rest. The feel of the softness beneath me, a comfort. The violence I'd seen earlier no longer pulsating against my psyche. My shoulders relaxed and my back muscles released the tension. I exhaled deeply and when I breathed in, the black warmth swallowed me.

My eyes flittered open, and I yawned, raising my arms above my head as I stretched. The white ceiling above me reminded me of a dentist's room. I jackknifed out of bed, unsure of my surroundings, then relaxed when I saw an office desk and chair with shelves lined with books.

Visions of those creatures fighting and being burned came to mind, and I shuddered at the memory. But I was safe, and we had won. I hoped.

I wiped the sleep out of my eyes and yawned. I glanced around the room again; desk, chair, books, and a corkboard filled with a large map and lots of little pieces of paper with fine print. Standing up, I stretched and headed for the corkboard.

Pushing papers out of the way, I noticed the map was of Earth showing the various continents and a large ice wall surrounding it. Then on either side of Earth were other continents or worlds. One would think those worlds were planets and far away, yet on this map they were right next door. And beneath our world were the world's River and I had traversed through to get to Mother Nature.

I read the post-it notes and its sightings for the creatures controlled by Seth. These creatures were all over the Earth, causing chaos wherever they were.

The floor shook, and I reached for the desk. I flinched when the door swung open with River standing in the door-jamb. "Good, you're up." He smiled and reached for me. "Let's go, the show's about to start." Before we left, he snaked his fingers through my hair and brought me in for a soft chaste kiss; it was short and sweet but filled with so much heat. If we were here under other circumstances, I was sure we would use the office for carnal pleasures, making me smile in our kiss.

He removed his hands from my body and reached for my hand. We exited the office, and he led me down a dark ice corridor, up a flight of stairs and into a viewing room of sorts. People filled the room, all staring out of the large window.

We stopped near a group of people, and I squealed with happiness. Blaire, my mom, spun around, pulling me into a hug.

"Oh baby, I'm so glad you're okay."

"Hey Mom. When did you get here?"

"A short while ago." She let go of me and I hugged Ralph and then Zenon.

"Hey lil' sister," Zenon said, knuckling my head gently. "How's the noggin doing?"

I swatted his hand away. "I'm fine," I said, smiling and giving him a second hug. It felt good to have my family with me, especially after the tumble I'd taken. It relieved me I could function after the things I'd seen. I let go of Zenon and snaked my arm around River's waist and nestling myself under his arm and against his side. I exhaled with relief and enjoyed the moment of his warmth embrace. He kissed the top of my head, and I could just melt.

"Are you feeling better?"

I glanced up, rocked onto my toes, and kissed him. "Yes, much better. How are you?"

"I'm fine," he said, kissing me chastely.

"What's everyone looking at, and why are they here?" I glanced at them again and they were staring at something outside.

"The war between good and evil has started."

"What do you mean?"

"After you went to sleep, Victor arrived demanding Seth show himself. And you won't guess who it was."

I shrugged. "Who?"

"Henry." I stared at him, open-mouthed. "I know, right? Anyway, so Seth was controlling his minions in his town all along. And now the brothers are about to fight one another."

The door flew open and in waltzed Os and Ossie. "Scout!" They yelled at the same time. I let go of River and approached them, and the brothers sandwiched me between them.

"You're here too."

"Of course," Ossie said, "we wouldn't miss it for the world."

Julia entered with a smile on her face. "Hey sister," she whispered, "glad you're up. Are you feeling better?" She smiled kindly.

I let go of the brothers and hugged Julia. "Hey yourself. I'm fine. When did you get here?"

"A few minutes ago, but you were asleep, so we checked out this block of ice," she said with a wicked wink, then her eyes found Os, her mate. He came in behind her, resting his chin on her head. "And now this demon wants popcorn for the fight."

A blast sounded, making me flinch. I let go of Julia and headed back to River and my family. I pushed in between Zenon and Ralph and glanced down; outside in the snow stood two enormous figures; Seth and Victor.

Chapter Twenty-Four

My father and uncle were each in their hellish forms; large build, black wings, dark horns, and glowing red eyes. They were sons of the same father; a man, but the worst devil ever known. But where my father was cunning, his brother was sinister, wicked, villainous, diabolical.

My father collected souls and sent them where they belonged.

Seth controlled creatures he had created. He tortured anyone he thought deserved it. He inflicted the worst kind of pain upon those who crossed him. And he always wanted to destroy my father. Not forgetting his search for Mother Nature and wanting to hurt her, too.

The door opened behind me, and another man walked through; short, black hair, and the darkest eyes I'd ever seen.

"Who's that?" I whispered.

Ossie was the closest and answered. "That's Maddox, Seth and Mother Nature's son."

My mouth opened in a surprise *O*. "So that's what he looks like." He reminded me of Seth.

"Yep, that's him," Ossie whispered. "He relinquished his duties with the help of your mother. She transposed his powers to his brother, who is the lesser devil of the two." He jerked his chin in Mom's direction. "Which only made Seth angry even more. But…" he shrugged, "by doing that, he ensured Seth left him alone. So, it all worked out in the end."

"Oh," I said, still staring at the dark, broody man, and then at Mom. I made a mental note to ask her about what she had done for Maddox.

Maddox crossed the room and draped his arm around Mother Nature. When she saw who it was, her face lit up, and she wrapped her arms around him. I loved family reunions.

A blast from outside shook the room we were in, pulling my attention back to the fight. The moment I turned to look outside, both men had doubled in size, and their sinister forms were that much more menacing. If any human was witnessing this fight, I was sure they would crumple into a pile on the floor, unable to process the events.

"No powers," Seth said in an ominous tone. "That's only fair."

"That's because your powers are no match for mine," Father said, puffing out his chest. His large black wings flapped behind him. "You've tried to destroy me for the last time, brother." He filled his deep tone with an extra hint of evil that I felt in my bones, making my arms pebble. "I've had enough. I think it's fair I give you what you've given me."

Victor didn't wait for Seth to respond. He spun around as if he was about to kick him, but instead of attacking, the circle he'd drawn in the snow glowed and something flew out of the portal before it closed again.

Victor stood still. Seth stood in a fighting stance. And the creature that had flown out of the portal flew overhead. I couldn't make out what it was until it landed beside Victor.

The figure wore the purest white dress stitched in gold. Her large white wings were greater than Father's black wings, and she glowed. The hairs on my body stood up, and I shivered. She was majestic in all her heavenly splendor.

"Who is that?" I asked no one in particular.

"That's Gabriella," Ossie said, "she's God's messenger."

"You can't involve her," Seth said, glowering.

"You lost the right when you had the Mask of Immortality slapped on my face."

"I want Father here. He'll put an end to this—"

Before Seth could finish his sentence, their father appeared between them. He was in his much older human form, clutching a walking stick. "Son, you disappoint me," he said, looking at Seth. "I've given you ample opportunities to resolve your issues with your brother civilly, and I specifically instructed you not to harm him. Yet," he coughed for effect, "you did. And you almost killed him... again. So," he nodded in the angel's direction, "she will teach you the lesson I never could, because if I leave Victor to do it, you will not survive. Know that this is in your best interest, son." And then he disappeared, leaving tiny bubbles popping in his wake, followed by female laughter.

"You have your answer," Victor said, stepping backward.

"No," Seth seethed, stepping forward and slapping his thigh. Something barked and slobbered and appeared by his side. It looked like a cross between a Rottweiler and a Pit Bull Terrier. It pulled its cut ears back, wore a black collar around its thick neck and a spiked muzzle. It was the biggest dog mix I'd ever seen.

Seth reached down and removed the muzzle. The Rottweiler/Pit Bull mix grew double in size, its eyes glowed red, and its sharp, toothy jaw snapped open and shut. Spittle flew everywhere when it barked and trained its eyes on Victor.

"It's over, Seth. Either bow down gracefully, or I will destroy you. Remember, I have dad's blessing."

"Attack!" Seth yelled and his demon-dog lunged for Victor, but Gabriella was there in a flash and touched the dog mid-air. The dog dropped to the ground, ran around Victor, and came to sit beside Gabriella. She patted him on his head and whispered, 'good boy'. He licked her hand and sat obediently with her. "No! What did you do to my dog?"

"All she needs to do is touch you, Seth," Victor said, stepping forward. "You know it's the best thing for you right now."

Seth shook his head, stepping away from Victor and farther away from Gabriella. "No, I'll fight before…" he left his words hanging and lunged for Victor wielding a knife in his hand.

Victor slammed his fist into Seth's jaw, stepped out of his grasp, and elbowed him in his back. Seth fell to the ground and spat out dark blood, staining the snow beneath him.

"Stay down, Seth," Victor warned.

"You know I'll never do that, brother," he said 'brother' with so much venom, I sensed Seth would rather die than have Gabriella touch him.

Seth levitated and flew into Victor. They crashed into a parked vehicle, crumpling it like tinfoil, but only Victor stood up. Seth moved onto his side and spat more dark blood into the snow. He reached for the wound on his right-hand side, pulling out the dagger with a red hilt that glowed. As Seth removed the dagger, the glowing hilt dimmed.

"What was that?" Seth said, throwing the dagger at Victor's feet.

"Let's just say they charmed it," he said, grinning. He approached Seth and crouched. His dark wings opening and covering them. Victor said something to Seth that made him flinch. He kicked his feet to get away from Victor, but Dad stood up and stepped away. The look on Seth's face said it all; whatever Dad had said, struck a nerve with Seth. I'd never seen him afraid of anything before.

"What was in that hilt?" I asked, glancing at Ossie. He was the boffin in the family, and he knew everything there was to know about the Underworld since he ruled over the library.

"If I had to take a guess," Ossie said, thinking, "it's one of Seth's daggers he had charmed himself. If I'm right, he just sentenced himself to a lifetime of torment in one of his levels in the Underground."

"He would rather go there than have an angel touch him?"

"Yep, stubborn fool," Ossie said, stepping away.

I glanced over my shoulder to see where he was going. Ossie approached Maddox, who slapped him on his shoulder. He whispered in Maddox's ear and the two half-brothers grabbed Os, and they exited.

"I wonder where they're going?" I said to River.

"Probably to your father and to say goodbye to Seth."

The three demons walked through the snow like the bad boys they were and stood beside Victor. Maddox crouched, said something to his father and stood up again. The expression on Seth's face changed and if I didn't know any better, he was ashamed.

Gabriella approached the men, her body glowing brilliantly against the snow. The dog walked by her side and waited patiently; no longer the hungry demon-dog. She said something to Victor, who glanced up at us with smiling dark eyes. He nodded and said something back to her. She kneeled before Seth, raising her hands above his wound. The dark blood pooled beneath him, draining him, but whatever she was doing seemed to restore something because his dark blood changed to the usual bright blood I was used to seeing.

Seth's dark features morphed into his human form, and he collapsed into the snow. His wound had healed, and he was now fully human.

Maddox picked up his father and carried him into the snowstorm. He whistled, and the demon-dog ran after them.

Everyone watched the two men head into the storm until they disappeared.

"Wow, what just happened?" I asked, breaking the silence.

"Maddox will look after his human father," River said.

"How do you know?"

"Your dad told me," he jerked his chin at my dad.

"Now?"

River faced me and smiled. "What do you think?"

"Ah, must be telepathy."

"Must be." He grinned.

Chapter Twenty-Five

I pulled the ticket out of my jacket pocket and showed it to the ticket agent near the door. Smiling sweetly when he grunted his approval, he handed me my half of the ticket back, and I pocketed the stub before entering the theatre.

Once I found my seat, I sat down, waiting for the show to begin.

The magician walked onto the stage, his black coat no longer shined or billowed behind him. He combed his fingers through his unwashed hair, scratched his beard, and welcomed the audience.

Now that his assistant was no longer around to help him with magic, he performed a basic card trick anyone could do, but his hands fumbled, and the cards fell to the floor. He mumbled under his breath, ignoring the cards, and pulled a napkin out of his pocket. The napkin changed colors from white to blue to green to pink to orange until eventually the last color, black, then he stuffed the entire napkin into his hand.

A man in the front row threw his ticket on the ground,

grumbled, and exited. The person in the sixth row followed him, also mumbling what a waste of money the show was.

The magician wiped his brow and performed a hat trick. When his hat tumbled out of his hands and landed on the floor, he kicked it farther away instead of picking it up.

Someone yelled 'boo', followed by more people leaving. There was commotion behind the closed doors, and it sounded like they wanted a refund.

The magician left the stage and came back with a rabbit. He belched as he placed the rabbit inside a glass cage and raised a saw. He swayed slightly, closing one eye as he tried to get the saw in the right spot.

A woman screamed, making the magician flinch.

"Stop! You're awful. Give me the poor animal before you kill that too, like your career," a man said from somewhere in the back. He stood up and ran down the stairs to the stage. "I think you've done enough, don't you think so, magician." The man held out his hand, silently asking for the animal.

The magician's cheeks reddened, and he hesitantly placed the saw on top of the glass cage. He glanced at the rabbit and then at the man. His shoulders dropped, and he opened the cage. The rabbit took that as an opportunity and jumped out, hopping toward the man near the stage.

The magician watched everyone leave but didn't notice me. When he started packing up, I clapped slowly, ensuring it echoed. He flinched, spun around, and squinted in the light to see where the noise was coming from.

"Did you think I wouldn't find you?" I said, standing up.

He scowled. "You ruined my life," he yelled, picking up the saw.

"Put that down if you want to live," I said, slowly making my way down the stairs toward the stage. "Or rather, if you want your soul to go to a nice place." I grinned.

"What?" the magician said, glancing nervously around. "Is your father here?"

"No, but I am," River said, crossing the stage toward him.

The magician backed away from River and when he burst into flames, the magician ran off the stage. He grunted as he bounced back onto the stage. Os and Ossie entered from the side curtain and towered over the magician in all their demon rage.

I neared the magician, who was now lying in the middle of the stage. I pulled a face when the stench of urine assaulted my senses.

"Please, please, I only did what he asked me to do."

"You betrayed the wrong demon, magician," I said, picking up his hat. "You won't be using this where you're going."

"No! Wait! Please, please," he cried.

I turned and headed back up the stairs, not needing to look over my shoulder at what my demon brothers were doing to him. Until he screamed. I glanced over my shoulder in time to see River remove the magician's larynx, silencing him, while the demon brothers dug their dark talons into his chest, fighting over who got to eat his heart.

Chapter Twenty-Six

"My oh my," Mom said, grinning. "It feels good to be back."

"Now, Blaire," Ralph said, "don't be messing with these people." Then he burst out laughing. "Oh, who am I kidding, that's why we're here."

Like Os, Ossie, River, and I did yesterday in search of the magician, we used the secret tomb to go back to the past to destroy the lizards at Lake Hills Institute who had hurt poor Alec and every other kid they touched. When we were last here, we didn't know what to do or if we were powerful enough to get rid of these evil bastards, but now that we knew who we were dealing with, we could handle them. Plus, this time I brought backup.

We traversed down the stairs and headed for the front door.

"It feels like yesterday we were here," Mom said.

"But it was more like twenty," I said, reaching for the bell.

"Yep, and I guess what we're about to do now will help

the other Hilling child get their job earlier," Ralph said, smiling. "Although he was just as creepy."

"The entire family is creepy. But I suspect we'll be changing things for their future. Just as long as they don't hurt another child, I'll be happy," Mom said, nodding.

I rang the doorbell and the same nurse who had helped us before opened the door and sneered. "What do you want now?" she said.

"Your boss, now open up before we do it for you," I said, and it felt so good.

The nurse flinched as if I had smacked her and reluctantly opened the gate. I pushed past her and headed for the main office. The nurse ran past me, screaming for Isaac Hilling.

The lizard-human exited his office and when he saw us storm his corridor, he turned the other way and ran. We chased after him, but it was Os and Ossie who crashed into him.

"What do you do with the children?" I asked, as anger filled my veins. I slapped his face, prompting him to answer.

The demon brothers held Isaac between them, and he kept trying to morph into his lizard form, but something was preventing him. His human skin kept glowing like scales, only to go back to his normal human self.

"It's to feed the demons," Isaac finally said. "They love hearing their screams and drinking the blood of innocents after their ordeal; it's akin to drinking fuel for their souls. The demons need the screams and the blood to live enriched lives."

"Not all demons feed like this," Ossie said angrily. He slapped Isaac on his forehead, branding him with his palm. I pulled a face when the smell of burned flesh assaulted my nose, but the visual scar in the shape of a demon was pleasing.

Isaac screamed as Ossie's print continued burning into his head, with smoke wafting in the air. Isaac's human skin seemed to melt into him, reminding me of when plastic melted.

"Who feeds off this?" I asked.

"I suggest you answer her," Mom said, pressing the sharp point of her blade into his cheek, drawing blood.

Isaac groaned. "Just stop, please."

Mom relaxed, but just a tiny bit. I didn't think she wanted to give him a chance to attack us.

"It was mainly for Seth," Isaac said. His eyes flitting from me to Mom and lastly focusing on Ossie's eyes. "You, of all demons, should understand what it's like under his thumb. We had no choice. And he has my sister."

"Louise?" Mom asked.

"Yes," Isaac said, nodding once and closing his eyes. "He has kept her in a cage the last ten years and if we ever want her back, we had to torture the kids."

Mom lowered her arm, no longer wanting to slit his throat. "I'll meet Lu in the years to come. She tries to do right what went wrong here. The sooner she takes over from you, the better for everyone involved." Then she turned toward Ossie. "Can you rescue her from wherever Seth kept her?"

"There are dungeons he would keep prisoners to toy with so we can check there first."

"Good," Mom said, "'cause I'd hate to waste energy on this one." She tapper the blade against Isaac's head.

"Isaac!" someone yelled, running down the corridor.

We spun around in time to stop a large orderly from

biting one of us. He ripped his clothing off and shifted into his crocodile form.

"No, Brent. Don't!" Isaac yelled, trying in vain to stop him. "Stop!"

Brent didn't stop. He had morphed into his much larger crocodile form, opening his enormous jaw. Ossie let go of Isaac and morphed into his much larger and scarier demon form. His hands shifted into scythes, and before Brent could bite me, Ossie chopped off his powerful jaw. Blood sprayed all over me. Brent collapsed, hitting me in the face with one webbed foot, before crashing onto the floor. I screamed from the impact. And another crocodile turned the corner and started a high walk as he galloped toward us.

"Stop Eddie, stop. Please, we can't lose another one," Isaac screamed. "We've had enough loss." Eddie stopped, now halfway from us. He opened his jaw, hissing. "Good boy, Eddie. Stay," Isaac said. His shoulders dropping. "No more bloodshed. Get my sister here now and we'll turn things around, but promise me, Seth must never return."

"Don't worry, croco-noodle," Os said, patting Isaac on top of his head. "Seth won't ever come back."

I sincerely hoped that was the case. I didn't think anyone could handle another disastrous Seth-attack.

Mom sheathed her blade. "Good, I think it's time we go. You two ok to bring Louise back here?"

"Yep," Ossie said, grinning at Os. "Everything will be fine now."

Chapter Twenty-Seven

River sat across from me, raising his hand and extending his index finger. His flaming phalange lighting the candle. "There we go," he said, smiling. His brown-colored eyes twinkling with humor.

I raised my glass of water to toast. He lifted his glass of wine, and we clinked them together. "I know things have been difficult these last couple of months," I started, unable to find the words. After a moment's pause, I finally said, "I'm glad we gave it another shot."

"Me too, Peanut," River said, his eyes flitting from my face to my belly. "And here's to our new beginning with that tiny peanut right there. I can't wait to meet him—"

"Or her." I smiled.

"Or her," he said, agreeing.

It's been nine months since my father's ordeal and almost losing River for good. Once the dust had settled, River and I had sat down to discuss our future or if we even had one together. He confessed his love for me and would do everything he could not to lose me again. While I would work hard not punishing him for his mistakes, or to take it out on my father for what he had done to River. I would take each day as it came, try to live in the present, and hopefully our future would be brighter than it was before.

I winced, rubbing my enormous belly. "It's been a good nine months," I said, sipping on my water.

"And to think I couldn't have children."

"That's before you became ill and human for a day." The day Mother Nature had rescued River in the boat, and after the fight my father had with Seth, we had found our way to each other in the most delicious way. I would never forget that day our naked bodies rocked into each other in a bedroom inside of the ice wall.

River grinned like a naughty schoolboy. "Yes, well," he said, clearing his throat. "I blame you."

"Me? What for?" I teased.

"You ravaged my body... I didn't have time to find protection."

"Haha, well, you never thought you could have kids and besides, I don't regret it." And I didn't. So far, I enjoyed every moment of my pregnancy. We didn't know whether our baby would turn into a flaming skeleton like River, but it would have some kind of supernatural powers.

Luna ambled toward River and licked his hand. "I'm so glad she returned," he said, rubbing the top of her head. Once we had returned home, River called her name into the universe, thinking he had lost her forever. But the next day, she scratched at his door in the Underworld. We were relieved she was home. Father had said that because River had amnesia, he had also forgotten Luna and she became lost within the Underworld. Then, once he regained his memory and called for her, she returned.

"It wouldn't be the same without her," I said, laughing

at Luna, who licked River's face. Jake squawked outside, a comfort that my crows were nearby.

I winced again.

"Are you okay?" River said, standing up.

"I'm fine." I lied. Our baby was testing its feet out on my ribs. "Ow."

"Come, let me take you to—"

"Aaaah!" I screamed, pushing my chair backward and doubled over as much as my stomach allowed. I did that breathing thing they taught me. Sweat peppered my forehead when another kick made me wet myself.

"I think your water just broke," River said, dialing a number. "Hello? Yes, yes, it's happening." He was quiet for a moment. "Yep, now." He slammed his phone on the table and disappeared, returning with towels and water. "Your mom is on her way and she'll bring Mel with her."

I couldn't answer because I was trying to control my breathing. The pain shot up my spine and it felt as though the baby was clawing its way through my uterus with sharp blades.

"River," I breathed. I glanced up at him through my soaked hair. He approached and kneeled in front of me. His expression helped me to relax.

"It's ok, Peanut, I'm here. I'm not going anywhere."

"Last chance to leave before the milk bottles and diapers start."

"I'm staying, Scout. I love you and baby peanut, and I'm not going anywhere."

Chapter Twenty-Eight

I cradled Jessica in my arms and no matter what I did, I couldn't stop crying.

"Here," Mom said, handing me a glass of water.

"What's inside?" I asked, staring at the murky water.

"Just something to keep you from dehydrating."

I took the glass from her and enjoyed a sip. "It's nice and sweet." I finished the drink, not realizing how thirsty I was. I handed her my glass and kissed Jessica's head. She stirred as she slept peacefully in my arms.

"Mel has left," Mom said. Mel was a were-wolf shifter doctor who tended to all supernaturals in Sterling Meadow. She was the best. "And she sensed something in Jessica."

"What do you mean?"

"Well, how can I say this—"

"Just spit it out." I knew Mel had a sixth sense; in that she could detect something supernatural in others.

"Now that you've grown into your father's powers and with River holding so much of his power too, that Jessica already exhibits some of those qualities."

"Well, that can only be a good thing." I smiled, glancing down at my tiny bundle when she moaned, as if battling a wind. She started glowing, reminding me of River before he turned into his flaming skeleton. "Oh wow," I said, sitting upright with her still in my arms. "Did you see that?"

"Yep, this could be fun," Mom said, reaching for her. I handed Jessica to her, and she cradled her against her chest and patted gently on her back. Mom sang a lullaby while she helped Jessica burp, and the glow that surrounded her disappeared. "Seems her own flames may arrive when she's unhappy or in discomfort. I can't wait to see River's face when he sees this."

I giggled. That would be a wonderful sight to see; River trying to calm his child down before she exploded into her own version of his flames. "Haha, I can't wait."

"Your father discovered one of Seth's demons had opened a portal. Which explained why that demon-goat was in the secret tomb, the Hydra we destroyed, and why that village disappeared."

"And now?"

"They have taken care of it. And Lu is safe and at the Lake Hills Institute."

"Good, change things around there."

"And guess what Ossie discovered?" Mom said but didn't wait for me to answer. "They found a folder on your magician, Harry. Apparently, his parents placed him at the Institute thinking he was supernatural, but he was just an odd little boy who loved magic." Mom shook her head. "And they tortured him relentlessly."

"It would explain why he was the way he was."

"True, but it didn't give him the right to hurt others."

"I know, but it's awful what he went through."

Mom was quiet for a moment as she held Jessica. She smiled as she hummed a tune.

"How does it feel to be a grandmother?" I asked, anxiously awaiting her response.

"I love it," she beamed, kissing Jessica's temple. "And she's beautiful, my darling daughter. I'm very proud of what you've accomplished not only by helping your dad but by becoming a mother yourself. And I know River will take care of you two."

"I know, I'm a lucky girl."

"And take your time with her. Come back to work only when you're ready."

"Thanks, Mom," I said, and would take at least six months' maternity leave before considering going back to work. I knew time with her would fly and if I wanted another six months off, I'd do it.

Mom handed Jessica back to me and kissed my forehead. I said goodbye and snuggled into the bed with my daughter beside me. We drifted off to sleep dreaming of under worlds and other worlds, and a little girl who glowed like the sun.

Also By N Gray

www.vinci-books.com/twisted

Be careful what you summon… you just might get it.

After witnessing a murder, I performed a ritual that went
hilariously wrong. Now I'm trapped in hell with a devastatingly
handsome demon lord who seems determined to claim more than
just my soul.

Turn the page for a free preview…

Twisted: Chapter One

All I wanted was an envelope. One stupid envelope to send a birthday card to my cousin. Instead of finding an envelope, I found this... documents about things I should never know about. This could get me killed.

Ice filled my veins, sweat beaded my forehead as I slowly closed the drawer. At first I expected the typical screeching sound when metal scraped against metal and was thankful I barely heard it close and relieved nobody else would either.

"What are you doing in my office?" Desmond's voice boomed behind me. His tone filled with rage.

I froze, swallowed hard, and slowly turned around. I fisted my hands as I glanced up at his hard face, finding nothing loving or caring about his expression. It was all hard lines and cold features.

My mind raced with things to say, to spew excuses for being in his office, but there was nothing. He had caught me with my hands in his things.

"Ah..." I muttered, swallowing the rest of my sentence as he approached with purpose.

"I've told you never to come in here." He scowled as he gripped my upper arms, yanking me away from his desk. He squeezed tightly, sending bursts of pain up my shoulders; hard enough to leave bruises.

"I was looking for an envelope—"

"Why?"

"It's my cousin's birthday, and I wanted to send her something."

"You shouldn't have opened my drawers, Julia. Do you understand the magnitude of your disobedience?" he said through gritted teeth, and the muscles in his jaw ticked. I'd never seen him this angry before.

"Yes..." I whimpered, averting my eyes. "Please don't hurt me, Des. I saw nothing." I lied. Obviously, I'd never tell him I saw the documents with multiple replicas they sold in Bill's art gallery. And I definitely wouldn't tell him I saw the name of the artist they commissioned who forged the paintings.

"I'm disappointed, Jules. I really am." He shoved two fingers painfully into my chest, pushing me into his filing cabinet.

I moaned on impact.

He raised his hand, but before he could strike, his cell-phone sounded. "Huh, saved by the phone. Get out but don't go far."

"Yes, Desmond," I said meekly, hurried past him and closed his office door behind me.

I didn't want to stay outside his door and upset him further. Instead, I ran to our bedroom and closed the door quietly. I leaned against the door, pressing my palms against the cool surface, relieved I no longer stood in front of him and the object of his anger.

The other bruises had faded, replaced with new ones.

My emotions ran high, and I flinched every time he raised his voice.

His rage had worsened the last couple of weeks. Something at work was stressing him out, and he took it out on me. But this... this was my fault. I shouldn't have gone into his office. He warned me. I should've known better.

My breath hitched. My head throbbed as I pressed it into the hard door. The pain felt right. I deserved it, as I sucked in another breath—holding it. The moment I exhaled, I cried.

I needed to think.

Desmond had warned me never to enter his office without him being present, and that's exactly what I did. He wasn't home, and I thought I could quickly look for an envelope, but he'd come home before I found one.

The longer I thought about it, the more I realized there had to have been a silent alarm I'd triggered when I entered his unlocked office. He'd just left when he rushed back home. If he wanted me not to go inside, he should've locked it. But I'd never say that out loud.

I flinched when he knocked on the door. "Julia?" His tone wasn't as sharp as it was earlier. Perhaps he'd calmed down.

"Yes?" I whispered, squeezing my eyes shut.

The door handle turned as he opened the door, but I was leaning against it, keeping it closed. My eyes shot open as I turned around. The consequences of not opening the door would only make my situation worse. Slowly, I stepped away from the door. I barely had time to move out of the way when he pushed the door open, smashing it in my face. The impact threw me off balance and I fell backward, landing on my backside with a loud groan.

Pain shot up my spine from landing on my coccyx, and

my face ached while my eyes teared. My hand came away with blood; my nose didn't feel broken but it would be bruised.

Desmond stood in the doorjamb, his large body imposing and bathed in sinister shadows. He stepped forward, towering over me.

"You really shouldn't have gone into my office, Jules." His tone was deep and frightening. All the hairs on my arms stood on end.

"I'm sorry." I raised my left hand near my face on instinct; unsure if he'd hit me again or if he had thought I'd suffered enough. I never could tell.

"It's okay," he whispered. His change in tone kept me on high alert; it could mean anything. "It's going to be okay. I spoke with Bill and I made it right again. He won't punish you. And nothing bad will happen while I'm around. See, everything I do, I do it for you. Don't you love me when I do so much for you? When I care so deeply?"

I nodded, then flinched when he reached for my head, but instead of pulling my hair, he caressed my head. His touch filled with warmth and kindness, and I leaned into his hand. This was the Desmond I loved; the kind and gentle man.

"I saw nothing, Des. I promise. I really only wanted an envelope."

"I know, and it's okay. I found one for you, here." He handed me a white envelope. I took it with a shaky hand. "Next time, come to me first. You know I will go out of my way to get anything for you. Okay?" He reached for my hands and pulled me to my feet. "There you go. Put some ice on your nose to stop the bleeding," he said. His words were kind, but the undercurrent of his tone was not.

"How far are you with the books I gave you?" he asked,

placing both hands on my shoulders and applied just enough pressure. He pressed on the fading bruises that still hurt, but I dared not cower—he hated when I moved away from him.

"I'll get it done in two hours."

"Good." He squeezed my shoulders once more, then kissed my cheek. His stubble scratching my skin. "Thank you for doing it at short notice." His smile ticked to one side. I could tell he was toning down his irritation. "Bill is also grateful for what you do for the business. You have an hour to finish them."

"Okay," I whimpered. I made the mistake of asking for an extension, I learned my lesson and wouldn't ask for another one. I'd ensure I finished on time. "Must I make dinner?" I asked, averting my eyes.

"No, you can fix yourself a sandwich if you're hungry. No," — he shook his head, — "you'll eat a salad. Bread is bad for your waistline. I have a business dinner I need to attend now, so I'll be home late." He let go of my shoulders. I dared not look up while under the weight of his gaze. "And Julia, it's going to be all right." He pulled me into the curve of his body and kissed the top of my head. "Des always fixes your nasty messes."

Twisted: Chapter Two

Julie

I showered and scrubbed my body until I was red and rinsed thoroughly. The old bruises on my shoulders had darkened from Desmond squeezing so hard, but at least I could cover it with a three-quarter sleeve top. I applied makeup to the already fading bruise on my cheek and my friend Bailey wouldn't know the difference.

I double checked the work Desmond had left me, and it was complete and correct. I doubted he would find fault. I was thorough with my work and my books always balanced. But it never hurt to check.

I left a note on the kitchen counter in case he came home before me. But since he was attending a late dinner meeting, I didn't think he'd come home before ten.

My friend Bailey had asked for an early dinner since we hadn't seen each other in over a month. She said she had good news for me. I needed to hear something good—especially today. I wanted to forget about my life. Listening to her was just what I needed.

I arrived at *Magic & Beans*, one of the best coffee shops in Sterling Meadow, found a parking spot near the entrance, and climbed out of my car.

Bailey sat at one of the outside tables and waved as I approached.

"Hey, hun. How are you holding up?" she asked, bringing me in for a hug. Her hugs were always exactly what I needed; filled with warmth, safety, and comfort. The smell of spring flowers and camomile tea wafted near her. She stiffened in our embrace and I wasn't sure what I did wrong.

"I'm fine—"

"No, you're not," she said, pulling away. "Something happened again, didn't it?" She held my shoulders and squeezed. I winced and tried to step away, but she held on. Her hands warmed. Her heat touched my skin through my clothing and burned down my arms.

"Ow," I moaned as my shoulders ached, followed by pins and needles shooting down to my fingers.

"He grabbed you again, didn't he?" She let go and sat down. A scowl crossed her usual pleasant features, and I knew she was mad.

I sat across from her, still rubbing my arms. My skin tingled as my neck and cheeks heated.

"I hate how you can sense things."

"I'm an excellent witch," she said with a smile and kind eyes.

"Nice hair. When did you have it done?" Last week her hair was lime green, today it's electric blue, reminding me of a mermaid I'd once seen when I was a kid.

"You like?" she asked, twirling a strand around her finger.

"Beautiful," I beamed at my friend. I was grateful to have her in my life. No matter my mood, she always made me feel better.

I told her about my work, avoiding the 'Desmond subject'. I knew how she felt. We had this discussion many times before. I didn't want to have it again.

Bailey told me about adding a few more clients to her 'consulting' business; a business where she helped others exact revenge on those who were deserving; mostly adulterers and bullies.

Bailey had potent spells she'd give to her clients to use on their 'target' which taught them a lesson. Nobody died, and it was never permanent. But it made her clients feel in control of their lives and boosted their self-confidence and morale.

I laughed uncontrollably when she told me one client mispronounced the name and her 'target' ended up with a wolf's tail for a month.

She also had clients who came to her for readings, and Bailey only used her gifts for good and empowerment; never for evil doing.

After we ate and enjoyed dessert, Bailey picked up her coffee and stared at me over the rim of her mug. I knew what she was dying to ask, but I always avoided the subject. We did not discuss Desmond... ever.

My relationship with Desmond was never this volatile before. I couldn't help but think it was partly my fault; I pushed him when I shouldn't and he was always nice to me afterwards. Bailey hated that. She said he was manipulative and abusive.

"I can't do this anymore, Jules. The man is going to kill you one day," she whispered, so only I heard. The nearby patrons too preoccupied with their own conversations. I doubted anyone cared about ours. "I know he sometimes has you followed," she continued, but her lips barely moved from behind her mug—reminding me of ventriloquists. "I've been thinking about this for a while and may have found a way of protecting you." Her eyes danced across the other patrons enjoying their late lunches. Then she turned her deep brown eyes on me, boring into my soul. "If Desmond threatens you, or you seriously fear for your life. I've already prepared the spell for you." She handed me a crumpled piece of paper, alerting no one to the fact. "Just say the words."

I chewed on my thumbnail as I read the words. "I'm not a witch. How will the incantation work for me?" I asked, although I wasn't sure I wanted to say the words anyway. Being with Desmond was comforting. Sure, he had his bad days, we all did. I didn't think I could have someone hurt him.

"The Demon Lord owes me a huge favor and he'll come to you the moment you summon him by saying the words. He will protect you with his life, Julia. When I say he owes me, *he owes me*." She arched both eyebrows. "He'll do what's necessary to get you out of there safely. If it's what you want. You do want it, don't you?"

I shrugged. My chest tightened at the thought. Desmond wouldn't let me go, he wouldn't allow me to just leave, especially since I did so much for his company.

Bailey sensed my conflicting emotions.

"It's the only way you can get away from that asshole," she grumbled. "You know he isn't good for you, and I know you're scared. He will stop you from leaving him. Abusers are like that. They manipulate you into thinking you need them. But you don't. You have me and you can stay with me again." She exhaled, red blotches marked her face as her anger slowly seeped away. "Next time he'll kill you." Her eyes flitted to my shoulders; the bruises hidden by my clothing.

I knew her words were true, but I still needed to believe them. It was hard for me to comprehend I could continue without Desmond. That I could get back on my feet. And being alone wasn't the same as lonely, but a choice to remove myself from harm. I knew all this... but... I struggled... perhaps with Bailey's help, I could.

"If I say these words, will the Demon Lord kill him?"

She shrugged. "He can, and he might. If Desmond tries to stop you from leaving, he will." She finished her coffee and set her mug on the table. She crossed her arms and gave me a deadpan expression.

She had thought this through. It was clear she hated Desmond. I loved him. But he scared me. He had hurt me a few times, but nothing so serious I needed a trip to the emergency room. Yet.

Desmond had anger issues that would trip him up quickly, but he always said '*sorry*' afterwards and begged for forgiveness. He was always sincere in his apology. I knew he loved me.

I glanced at the crumpled paper again, unsure how a Demon Lord could help, but I'd hold on to it. I tucked it into my jean pocket and sipped my coffee.

When the clock struck eleven, Desmond still hadn't come home.

I'd just fallen asleep when the front door opened and slammed shut. I waited for him to enter our bedroom and to assess his mood, but after two minutes had passed, he didn't show.

There were strange murmurs somewhere near the front of the house. Then muffled voices set my alarm bells off. I couldn't tell if they were arguing or just speaking in hushed tones.

I pulled on my robe and opened the bedroom door.

"Desmond?" I called above a whisper.

"Oh, hey," Desmond said as he entered the hallway so I could see him, then he added, "Bill's here." He thumbed behind him.

A dark shadow moved behind Des. I froze to the spot and reached for my upper left arm, feeling the scar. A deep scar Bill had inflicted with his sharp claws when I tried to walk away from him while he was speaking. He didn't appreciate anyone walking away from him. He taught me a lesson by inflicting pain and leaving me a memento; every time I saw him, I'd remember what he did.

I sucked in a deep breath.

"Hey, Bill. How are you?" I said as I calmly traversed down the hallway towards them.

"Julia!" Bill's tone was ominous and struck a chord within me, leaving me speechless. He licked his bloody lips. My eyes flitted from Bill's mouth to Desmond's neck; the wound already healed by vampire saliva.

Desmond was a blood-servant for Bill only. In exchange for being a regular blood donor, Desmond received other benefits; improved health, longevity, a salary and security; all this for a few sips of blood a few times a week.

Desmond rubbed his crotch. His eyes darkened as his pupils dilated—no doubt Bill's bite was sensual. I was sure there was something else going on in their *work* relationship, but I never asked. I doubted they'd tell me anything, anyway.

Bill wanted me to be his blood-slave, too, and I refused him without thinking about it. I didn't want to be passed between masters in exchange for their addictive blood. I'd never tasted vampire blood before, nor would I ever—if I could help it.

"Desmond says you might have read something belonging to me?"

"I was only looking for an envelope."

"And did you find one?" Bill asked, arching a black eyebrow. Bill was a head taller than me, with black hair and eyebrows, and gray/silver eyes. His skin was pale and his features sharp. He hardly showed any emotions, which kept everybody on edge. Even Desmond.

My eyes flitted to Desmond, then back to Bill as his dark gaze raked up and down my body. I hated how he did that—making me uncomfortable by his stare alone—and so quickly.

"Ah, no, but Desmond came home and found one for me," I said, wiping my palms on my gown. My smile wavered at the sides and I knew Bill sensed my fear. I suspected my fear had a sour smell to it; I stood before Bill many times and knew I smelled like that every time.

"What did you see, Julia?" Bill's tone was crisp and unforgiving as he stepped closer. Dark shadows played on his features, his eyes seemingly more metallic than gray.

Instinctively, I stepped backward. But Bill was too fast for me. I barely saw him move. He gripped me by the throat and shoved me against the wall. I clutched at his wrist, trying to pull his hand from my neck. He squeezed until my pulse thundered in my ears. I couldn't breathe. My eyes bulged. Stars clouded my vision. Bill's features morphed as the darkness swept over him, leaving his true, twisted, demonic self.

I glanced at Desmond, who stood behind Bill with his arms folded over his enormous chest, wearing a smile, his dark eyes glistening; he was just as twisted as his boss.

"Please," I breathed. My vision tunneled. Darkness swarmed around me. My chest ached. And my head felt as though it was about to pop off.

Bill finally let go and I crumpled to the floor. My limbs were numb and unable to keep me up as I landed with my butt on the floor and slumped against the wall. I sucked in a deep breath. Slowly, my limbs came alive and I rubbed my aching neck.

"It's only because Desmond loves you I haven't killed you already, *human*. I don't like it when someone snoops in my drawers."

I already knew it was Bill's drawers because of the documents with the painter's name and the paintings he'd forged.

"Ah, there we have it. You've realized, haven't you? So you did read inside—"

"I didn't I swear. I saw nothing. And if I did, I wouldn't say anything to anyone." I hated how my face sometimes gave me away.

They took part in organized crime, and it was lucrative. I suspected if anybody tried to intercept, Bill would have them dealt with swiftly. But what bothered me the most, with modern dating and analysis techniques, surely it would make the identification of forged artwork that much simpler. The people buying these paintings most likely trusted Bill blindly, or there's another reason, possibly money laundering.

"I know." Bill crouched in front of me; his aftershave assaulting my senses along with that copper stench. He reached for my face and I dared not move or he'd rip my throat out so quickly I wouldn't know what hit me, then he'd lap up my blood. "So pretty, and so clever, especially that memory of yours." He tapped the side of my head.

I pulled away then. I hated when someone tapped me on my head. It reminded me of school when the bullies hit me, taunted me, and sang, *'Dumb-dumb, Julia is a dumb-dumb.'* I was not stupid. School bored me. I knew every word in every textbook and could recite it word for word. All they had to do was give me the page number, and I'd tell them. But I was also lazy and never did my homework.

"Don't do that—"

"She hates it," Desmond said, tapping Bill on his shoulder. "She won't say anything. Will you Jules?"

I shook my head but kept my eyes on Bill. His eyes glowed red, and I was sure I wet myself; I couldn't be sure since my body felt numb.

"Go to bed. And if I hear you've done something like this again, I'm coming for you." Bill promised, and stood up in one swift motion. But he didn't move away. He towered over me like the dangerous vampire he was, ensuring I never forgot his threat.

———

I did as instructed and ran to our bedroom, slamming the door shut. I jumped into bed, covered my body with the duvet, and cried until I fell asleep.

My dreams came soon thereafter, and they were always the same…

I sat at my favorite coffee bar, Alpha Coffees, enjoying a cappuccino and a bran muffin when Desmond entered the shop. His charming smile held promise of something more, something dangerous yet alluring.

He couldn't tear himself away as his eyes raked up my body, leaving me hot and bothered.

Nobody had ever looked at me that way. He set all the alarms within me ringing and I didn't want him to stop. I didn't heed the warning.

Once he had placed his order, he asked if he could sit at my table. I graciously agreed; we had greeted each other before but this was the first time he joined me at my table. We spoke about anything and everything.

Desmond was an influential businessman, and I had just started working at an accounting firm. He grinned when he told me he needed an accountant and asked if I wanted to earn double my current salary. I almost choked on my coffee.

If I earned double my salary, I could pay off my student loans quicker and save for a house of my own. Living with my witchy roommate was wonderful, and we had fun, but it was still her apartment. I wanted a place of my own.

Desmond promised me the moon and so much more.

I was full of smiles with plans of my own and agreed to join Desmond's company.

The first week was wonderful. His books were easy to balance, and I saved him money on his taxes.

To celebrate, Desmond took me out to a French restaurant and ordered the most expensive food and drink. We ate, drank champagne, and spoke all night long. He was so romantic and kind. Before I knew it, I was in his bed, screaming his name.

Two days later, I moved in with him.

But by then it was too late.

Being the honest and trusting person my parents had taught me to be…

I didn't see the warning signs.

Grab your copy…
www.vinci-books.com/twisted

About the Author

A Multi-genre author writing twisted endings...

N Gray is a USA Today Bestselling Author who lives in Cape Town, South Africa, with her daughter and adopted cat named Miss Beans.

During the day, she's an analyst and provider profiler for a medical insurance company. At night, she types on her curved keyboard, creating fictional characters some may love and others you want to kill yourself.

She writes in four genres: urban fantasy, thriller, horror, and paranormal romance.

She now writes under Natalie Michaels for her new thrillers and SD Syns for her new horrors.

Acknowledgments

Thank you to my readers, old and new, for taking a chance on my books.

You are the reason I write the stories I do. As long as you keep reading, I'll keep writing.

I'm truly humbled by your support and encouragement.

I write in as many genres as I love reading in. There are so many stories swarming inside my head that I could never just choose one.

Horror is my guilty pleasure. I love writing short stories filled with dark humour and the occult with a twist ending.

Urban fantasy and paranormal romance are where I love to spend my time, and I have so many books planned that I don't have enough time (*but I'll get there*).

And lastly, my thrillers. Who doesn't love sitting on the edge of their seat while reading about what goes on inside the antagonist's mind? Well, I love writing about them.